MASSACRE RIDGE

MASSACRE RIDGE

LEWIS B. PATTEN

THORNDIKE
CHIVERS

This Large Print edition is published by Thorndike Press®, Waterville, Maine USA and by BBC Audiobooks Ltd, Bath, England.

Published in 2005 in the U.S. by arrangement with Golden West Literary Agency.

Published in 2006 in the U.K. by arrangement with Golden West Literary Agency.

U.S. Hardcover 0-7862-7960-5 (Western)
U.K. Hardcover 1-4056-3577-0 (Chivers Large Print)
U.K. Softcover 1-4056-3578-9 (Camden Large Print)

The text of this Large Print edition is unabridged.
Other aspects of the book may vary from the original edition.

Set in 16 pt. Plantin by Ramona Watson.

Printed in the United States on permanent paper.

British Library Cataloguing-in-Publication Data available

Library of Congress Cataloging-in-Publication Data

Patten, Lewis B.
    Massacre Ridge / by Lewis B. Patten.
      p. cm. — (Thorndike Press large print westerns)
    ISBN 0-7862-7960-5 (lg. print : hc : alk. paper)
    1. Sioux Nation — Fiction. 2. Wyoming — Fiction.
3. Large type books. I. Title. II. Thorndike Press large
print Western series.
PS3566.A79M373 2005
813'.54—dc22   2005015303

X000 000 020 9439

MASSACRE
RIDGE

CHAPTER 1

At eight in the evening, Jess Paddock stepped out into the bitter wind howling down out of the Bighorn Mountains half a dozen miles west of the fort. The post buildings and the eight-foot log stockade failed to break its sweep and Paddock had to lean into it as he walked. He passed the guardhouse and the unfinished post head-quarters building and entered the sutler's store. He had just left a poker game in the NCO quarters at the east end of Laundress Row. His pockets were comfortably heavy with his winnings but his pleasure was tempered by memory of Sergeant O'Mara's fiercely scowling, reddened face. O'Mara was a poor loser and he had come close to accusing Paddock of cheating him.

The sutler's store was as warm as any building at Fort Phil Kearny. It smelled of the pine sawdust on the floor, of whisky and cooking odors and of men. A bluish layer of tobacco smoke hung close to the ceiling, which consisted of rough-sawed pine boards laid over peeled pole ceiling joists. Jess Paddock crossed quickly to the bar.

A few enlisted men were here, those still having something left out of their pay. Five civilians had a poker game going at a table against the wall. The post sutler's agent, John Kinney, was behind the bar. Paddock said, "Whisky, John."

Kinney brought glass and bottle and Paddock poured his own. He drank it quickly, feeling still the chill of the bitter wind, and perhaps some uneasiness because of O'Mara's rage. Kinney asked, "Been playing poker, Jess?"

Paddock nodded, a rueful grin touching the corners of his mouth.

Kinney asked, "What are you grinning at? O'Mara?"

Paddock nodded. "He's a sorehead. He thinks he always ought to win."

"Don't laugh *him* off. He's mean and he's dangerous."

"I know."

Paddock poured himself another drink, but he slowly sipped this one. He was a big and broad-shouldered man, seeming even bigger in his heavy, sheepskin-lined winter coat. Warmed, he now unbuttoned it.

He wore a gray Confederate cavalry officer's hat with the insignia removed.

His eyes were as gray as the hat. His brows were shaggy and his face was deeply seamed by years and weather and hardships unquestioningly endured. He had helped Jim Bridger guide Colonel Carrington's fort-building force to this place between the forks of Piney Creek. He had stayed when Bridger left. There was a reason why he stayed. She was a widow and she lived in the second hut on Laundress Row.

Kinney said, "There's something going on."

"What do you mean?"

"Colonel Carrington has had his officers over at his quarters for more'n an hour now."

"Maybe Fetterman and Brown have finally managed to talk him into an expedition against the Indians."

"Maybe. Most of the work on the fort is done. Everybody's out of the tents and the place is as secure as it will ever be."

Paddock said sourly, "And two thirds of the men are raw-assed recruits. None of them have fired a gun in months. The Sioux will eat them alive."

The door opened and Colonel Carrington's Negro servant, Black George, came in. He grinned when he saw Paddock and crossed the room to him. "The colonel, he wants to see you, suh."

Paddock downed his drink. He paid Kinney, nodded at George and, tugging at the brim of his hat and buttoning up his coat, followed him out into the darkness and the bitter wind.

The pair hurriedly crossed the snow-covered parade, passed the uncompleted quarters intended for the post's commanding officer and entered one of the smaller temporary officers' quarters occupied by Colonel Carrington and his family.

The living room was filled with smoke. Carrington and his officers were seated around its sides. Carrington came forward and shook Paddock's hand. "Glad George found you, Jess. I want you to be in on this."

Paddock glanced around at the officers, nodding to them one by one. There was Fetterman, whose permanent rank was captain but who was usually addressed as colonel, his brevet rank during the war. There was Captain Tenedor Ten Eyck, Captain Powell, Captain Brown, Lieutenants Bingham, Wands and Grummond. The post surgeon, Dr. Hines, was not present.

Paddock faced Carrington again. The colonel said, "As you know, there has been considerable pressure upon me to take the field against the Indians. So far, I have resisted it because it has been my conviction that completion of the fort before winter set in was of the first priority. However, since most of the buildings are completed and the others nearing completion, I have decided that it might be time for a limited offensive against the Sioux."

Paddock waited expectantly. Carrington said, "We have discussed it thoroughly. Let me outline the plan for you." Quickly he outlined that he would send out a wood cutting detail in the morning as usual. When it was attacked, as it almost invariably was, a force of cavalry under Col. Fetterman and Lt. Bingham, would ride to its relief. They would pursue the Sioux along the Indians' usual escape route, over the Sullivant Hills into the valley of Big Piney Creek, thence over Lodge Trail Ridge and down into the valley of Peno Creek.

Carrington would, at the same time, lead a force of mounted infantry straight north along the Bozeman Trail, staying east of Lodge Trail Ridge. He would come into Peno Creek from the east, hopefully catching the Sioux between his force and that of Fetterman.

Finished, he asked, "What do you think?"

Paddock hesitated, glancing around the room. Some of the officers were eyeing him warily. Brown was frowning, as was Fetterman. He said, "Might work, I guess, if all you got to contend with is the thirty or forty Indians that attack the wood detail."

Fetterman asked, "What do you mean by that?"

Paddock looked at him. "I mean that there are Sioux villages strung out along the Tongue River for nearly twenty miles. I've seen 'em myself. There must be several thousand fighting men in those villages, and no matter what else you might think of them, the Sioux are neither stupid nor cowardly."

Fetterman growled, "I could take a hundred men and ride through the whole damned Sioux nation."

Paddock didn't bother to answer him. Fetterman's eyes were glowing almost fanatically and his face was taut.

Carrington prodded, "What are you getting at, Jess?"

"If they've been baiting traps with their attacks on the wood detail . . ." Paddock stopped a moment. Then he asked, "Ever see coyotes lure a dog away from a farmyard,

Colonel? They'll send in a bitch and she'll whine and bark until the dog starts after her. She'll head off across a ridge, an' every time the dog starts back, she'll stop and lure him on again. Soon's he gets over the ridge he finds the pack waitin' for him. They tear that foolish dog to bits."

Fetterman said disgustedly, "That's ridiculous. Do you really think they've been setting a trap for us out there every day?"

Paddock corrected, "I didn't say they had. I said 'if they have.'"

Carrington said, "We'll take a sufficient force. Fetterman, you take at least twenty-five men from Lt. Bingham's company. I'll take another twenty-five mounted infantrymen. Paddock, I'd like to have you accompany me."

Captain Brown muttered something that Paddock didn't hear. Carrington glanced sharply at Brown. "What did you say?"

Brown said, "I'd like to go along with Col. Fetterman."

Carrington nodded. He knew that wasn't what Brown had said and so did Paddock. Paddock gave Brown a level glance that the captain met defiantly.

Carrington said, "I guess that's all then, gentlemen."

Immediately they rose and took their leave. Paddock went out into the bitter, driving wind and strode swiftly across the parade. The others took time to put on their greatcoats before venturing into the cold.

Light was shining through Molly Benedict's window. Paddock paused and stared at the beckoning square of light. It was only a little after half past eight. He turned and walked swiftly to the door. He knocked and a moment later the door opened.

Wind swirled in, stirring Molly Benedict's hair and skirt. She smiled and said, "Come in, Jess. Come in out of that awful wind. I think I have a little coffee left."

He went in, closing the door behind him. He removed his hat and unbuttoned his coat. "I won't stay. It's late."

"Stay for coffee. I was wishing you would come."

She was a strong and full-bodied woman in her early thirties. Her hair was dark, untouched with gray, and her face was high-cheekboned and smooth except for lines of good humor at the corners of her eyes. Her mouth was full and somehow sweet even when it held no smile. He had often felt sorry for her because of the way she had to work. He had seen her when she was very tired but he had yet to hear her complain. Her husband had been killed in a fight with another soldier at Fort Laramie. Without means of support and not wanting to return east, where she had no family anyway, she had come with Carrington's command as a laundress.

Paddock could remember the time, about a month ago, when he had asked her to marry him. She had studied him with an amused smile and had bluntly charged, "You just feel sorry for me."

He denied it, of course, but to himself he admitted she was right. He had been feeling sorry for her.

Still smiling, mocking him a little, she had said, "You're much too wild, Jess Paddock. I doubt I could tame you and I'm not sure I want to try."

Now he admitted he had felt somewhat relieved. She turned from the stove, coffeepot in hand, and looked at him. "What are you grinning about?"

"I was thinking about the night I asked you to marry me. Have you changed your mind?"

She shook her head. "You could never stay in one place for very long."

He studied her deliberately until she blushed. "I think it might be fun to try."

She avoided his eyes as she filled his cup. She filled her own and sat down facing him.

"Aren't you going to take off your coat?"

"It's late. I'm not going to stay."

Now it was her turn to study him. "Something's on your mind, isn't it? Do you want to tell me what it is?"

"Carrington's going to take the field against the Indians."

"When?"

"Tomorrow."

"Isn't that what everybody's been wanting him to do?"

He nodded.

"But it worries you. Why?"

He grinned. "You see too much in me."

"You needn't tell me if you don't want to."

"I don't mind. I just think that a lot of Carrington's officers, Fetterman particularly, fail to take the Sioux seriously."

"And you do."

"I do. This is their winter hunting ground. They have seen what happened to other tribes when they let the whites come in. They'll stand firm against this fort. They'll stand firm against the Bozeman Trail. And they can fight. When they want to, they can fight."

"But they have no guns."

"Not now they don't. But they have their lances and arrows and tomahawks. And

16

sooner or later, they'll have guns as well. If they have to kill soldiers to get them."

He finished his coffee and got to his feet. Her face was now concerned as she asked, "You are going out with them?"

He nodded.

She came to him and took his hand. "Be careful, Jess."

He bent and kissed her lightly. There was, unexpectedly, a new expression in her eyes, a vulnerable look he had never seen in them before.

She reached up, put her arms around his neck and drew his head down toward her. She kissed him firmly on the mouth.

His arms went around her and tightened, but she pulled away. "Go now, Jess. See me tomorrow before you leave."

He stood there hesitating a moment, confused, his blood pounding in his head. Then he put on his hat and went out the door. He closed it softly behind him, remembering her face and the look he had seen so briefly in her eyes.

He knew he wanted her. But did he want her enough to stop the wild, free wandering which was all he had ever known? Frowning, he headed for his bachelor quarters on the northeast side of the quartermaster's corral.

CHAPTER 2

Paddock's room was cold. He lighted his lamp, stirred the embers of the fire in his little potbellied stove and added several sticks of firewood. He stood close to the open door of the stove while the wood caught and only when it had did he close the stove and take off his coat.

His quarters consisted of a single twelve by twelve room built against the eight-foot log stockade that encircled the fort. The floor was of packed earth. The roof was close-laid poles over which dry prairie grass had been spread. Over that was a foot-thick layer of native clay. The log walls were chinked with the same clay and successfully kept out the wind. In the unlikely event that the Sioux attacked the fort, he had only to leap onto his roof from which position he could fire over the stockade at the attacking Indians.

The room warmed gradually. He could hear the wind whistling past the eaves. Intermittently it rattled the heavy plank door against its catch.

At nine-thirty, he added a couple of large pieces of firewood to the stove and removed his clothes down to his flannel underwear. He blew out his lamp, crawled into his blankets and pulled them up around his chin. He lay there, staring at the ceiling, listening to the wind for a while before he went to sleep.

He never knew exactly what awakened him. Some slight noise, perhaps, unusual enough to penetrate his sleep. He opened his eyes, lying quite still, listening. Instantly he knew someone was in his room. A faint glow of red came from the isinglass vent in the door of the stove. By this light he could see a bulky figure halfway between his bed and the door.

He heard the clink of coins and realized that whoever was in the room was going through his pants. He gathered his muscles and suddenly flung back his blankets and leaped from his bed. He reached the man in a couple of strides, striking him with a shoulder and encircling his thick body with his grappling arms.

The two, locked together, crashed against the door. Coins, dropped by the intruder, rattled against the log walls and rolled across the floor. The intruder cursed with startled surprise and tried to twist away.

He failed, Paddock hung on and the two struggled desperately, still locked together in a straining embrace. A heavily-booted foot came down on Paddock's bare one and he howled with pain. But he was angry now. He released the man, set himself and released a long, looping hard-clenched fist that caught the intruder on the cheekbone and sent him staggering against the stove.

It yielded with a crash, overturning and skidding across the earthen floor. It slammed against the far wall in a shower of sparks. The stovepipe came tumbling down immediately afterward, making a racket that, Paddock thought, ought to wake the dead.

The intruder fell on a carpet of scattered coals from the upset stove. They burned through his pants and he uttered a roar of pain and rage. And suddenly Paddock knew it was squat, burly Sergeant O'Mara, who had so resented losing his money earlier tonight in the poker game.

Forgetting the coals that littered the floor, he rushed toward O'Mara, who was trying to get to his feet and at the same time beat out the smoldering places in his pants. Paddock stepped on a red-hot coal and let out a shout of pain. Ignoring O'Mara now for a moment, he raised his foot and slapped at the coal stuck to its sole.

O'Mara chose that instant to let loose with a haymaker that must have started below his knees. It caught Paddock on the forehead and sent him crashing against the door. Stunned, he slid down into a sitting position in front of it. O'Mara tried to shove him aside so that he could open the door and escape, but Paddock locked his arms around the sergeant's knees and brought him tumbling to the floor.

The room was, by now, filled with smoke from the overturned stove. Paddock started to cough. The smoke burned his eyes and they streamed tears across his sooty cheeks. O'Mara was coughing too, but he was still frantically trying to get away.

Paddock felt a knife slash both his underwear and the muscles of his back and realized suddenly how deadly serious this had become. He released O'Mara's legs and plunged across the room toward his bed where his holstered revolver and belt hung from the bedpost.

Realizing what he was after O'Mara stopped, set himself and flung the knife. It thudded into the log wall a foot from Paddock's head. O'Mara followed, chopping at Paddock's head with his own hastily drawn service revolver.

Paddock yanked his gun from its holster and whirled, stepping on another coal as he did with the same foot he had burned before. It gave beneath his weight and he fell. At that instant O'Mara's gun blasted, its roar all but deafening in this small, enclosed area.

The bullet cleanly missed. On his back, still rolling, Paddock brought his gun to bear and fired.

He rolled onto a coal as the flash lighted the room and yelled again from the painful burn it made on his rump. He fought to his feet, thumbed back the hammer and roared, "Drop it you sonofabitch or I'll blow your goddam head off!"

O'Mara froze but he did not drop his gun. The door flung open and half a dozen men in their underwear crowded the opening.

O'Mara rushed them like a maddened bull. He bowled them aside like tenpins and disappeared into the darkness.

A couple of the men ran after him. Barefoot and wearing only their underwear, they soon turned back. Sentries began shouting excitedly from their platforms on the stockade.

The remaining men came crowding in. Paddock found the lamp, which was miraculously intact. He lighted it and stared around at the wreckage of his room.

Lieutenant Wands, apparently officer of the day, appeared in the doorway. "What's going on here? What's happening?"

Paddock knuckled his streaming eyes. He sat down on his bed and lifted his burned foot to stare at it. He said, "I woke up and found someone going through my pants."

"Who was it? Did you get a look at him?"

"Too dark and things were happening too damn fast."

Wands looked at his bleeding back, at the knife imbedded in the wall. He said, "I'll send Dr. Hines over to bandage up your back. Are you hurt anyplace else?"

Paddock shook his head. Wands left. The other men, all civilian teamsters, muttered their sympathy and backed out of the room.

Grumbling angrily, Paddock found a worn-out pair of gloves. He put them on and, walking carefully to avoid any more smoldering coals, righted the stove and put it back where it belonged. He put the sections of stovepipe together and connected it.

The room was icy now. With shaking hands, he laid another fire and lighted it. Shivering in his underwear, he stood close to the stove's open door until it began to throw off a little warmth.

Money was scattered from one end of the room to the other. His pants were smoldering. There were ashes and dead coals all over the floor. Muttering to himself, Paddock picked up his pants and pinched out the smoldering place. He gathered the money and put it back into his pants pockets. By the time he had finished, Dr. Hines was at the door.

The slash across Paddock's back, while painful, was not serious. The knife had not much more than cut through the skin. Dr. Hines put a compress over it, winding strips of bandage around Paddock's chest to make the compress stay in place.

He gave Paddock a small jar of salve for the burns. Finished, he sat down and looked at the mess the fight had made of the room. "I hear you won considerable from O'Mara tonight."

Paddock grinned at him.

"Couldn't have been O'Mara, could it?"

"If it was, he's got burns on his butt just like I have."

Hines grinned back at him. "Then all

you got to make him do is show his butt."

"There'll be more important things to think about tomorrow."

"What do you mean by that?"

"The Colonel has planned an offensive action against the Sioux."

"Probably a good thing. They're getting pretty bold."

"They can afford to be."

"Fetterman says he can whip the whole Sioux nation with a hundred men."

"Fetterman is a fool."

"Maybe. But he's been pretty critical of Colonel Carrington. So have the other officers."

"I think Carrington's done a good job. He wasn't sent here to fight Indians. He was sent to build a fort and he's built it."

"He hasn't drilled the men the way he should. They're sloppy and the discipline is terrible. I patch men up every day, men cut with knives and men battered with fists. The sutler's store was broken into three times last week."

"The men have been working. They've been building instead of soldiering. It took three thousand foot-thick logs eleven feet long to build the stockade. A trench three feet deep and half a mile long had to be dug. And besides that they've built barracks and commissary buildings and warehouses and latrines and your hospital and officers' quarters and stables and God knows what else. There's been no time for drill. Carrington knew he had to get everybody out of the tents before the worst of the winter set in. He made it and I think he deserves more credit than anybody is giving him."

Hines stared at him. "That's quite an impassioned defense."

Paddock growled, "Somebody's got to defend the man. He won't defend himself."

"What do you think of the offensive he's planned for tomorrow?"

Paddock shrugged. "Fifty men against the thousands of Sioux out there?"

"You think they'll all get killed?"

"I think they could."

"Are you going?"

Paddock nodded.

Dr. Hines got to his feet. "Then you'd better get some sleep," he said. He went to the door, buttoned his heavy coat and turned the collar up. He stepped out into the bitter wind and Paddock closed the door after him.

He didn't feel like doing any more cleaning up tonight. He put a couple of thick chunks of wood into the stove and closed the damper partway so that they would burn longer. He put some salve on his burns, blew out the lamp and got into bed for the second time tonight.

He didn't think O'Mara would be back. But just in case, he withdrew his revolver from its holster and laid it on the floor beside his bed.

For a little while, pain in his back and in his burns kept him awake. But at last he slept, and he did not awake until the clear notes of reveille sounded outside on the parade.

CHAPTER 3

Immediately after breakfast, the wood train assembled in the quartermaster corral. Two teams of mules were hitched to each heavy wagon. Civilian teamsters drove and each was assigned a soldier who could fire at attacking Indians while the teamster handled the lines. All of the teamsters carried rifles, and most had revolvers as well.

The departure of the wood train was an almost daily occurrence and usually attracted little attention. Today however, a number of men climbed up onto the three-foot-high banquette that ran along the inside of the stockade in order to watch the fifteen wagon wood train as it slowly followed the wood road along the base of the Sullivant Hills.

Soon the sounds of hammers, sledges and saws, the fort's normal, daily noise, began. About twenty-five men of Lt. Bingham's cavalry company assembled on the parade, along with an equal number of infantry, hand-picked by Lt. Grummond for the day's sortie.

Jess Paddock left the teamsters' mess in the quartermaster corral and turned toward the parade. He overtook Molly Benedict coming from the creek, carrying two pails of water. He took them from her, noting that despite the cold morning air, her smooth forehead was beaded with perspiration.

He carried the water into her quarters where a large wash boiler was already steaming on the stove. He put the buckets down and turned to find her smiling up at him. "If you keep carrying water for me people are going to talk."

He grinned back. "Let 'em."

"What is this I hear about you? A fight in your room last night?"

He said, "Someone took a notion to go through my pants. I objected and he got away. There's no more to it than that."

Her expression lost its mockery. "Nothing more to it than that? I heard mention of a knife and of a deep cut across your back."

"It wasn't as bad as that. The cut was just a scratch. The surgeon bound it up."

"Do you still intend to go out with Colonel Carrington after the Indians?"

"Nothing to stop me. My back's a little sore is all."

She nodded skeptically and began to

sort through a pile of laundry on the floor. Paddock left and continued his walk down the line of small log cabins that comprised Laundress Row.

Two enlisted men were coming out of one of the cabins that belonged to "Colored Susan," laundress for Company H, 2nd Battalion. They glanced guiltily at Paddock, then ducked their heads and hurried away.

Paddock grinned to himself, knowing that in all probability there would later be a report of the quartermaster storehouse being broken into sometime last night. Stolen articles would include dried fruit, flour, lard and other ingredients needed for baking pies. In addition to doing Company H's laundry, Colored Susan baked and sold pies to enlisted men, the pies being made from ingredients stolen from the quartermaster's stores. Susan also sold liquor, though it was not known where she obtained it. Probably it was smuggled to her by friendly teamsters from Fort Laramie.

Susan appeared in the doorway of her cabin and grinned cheerfully at Paddock as he passed. She was an ample woman with a face that was shiny and very black. She called, "Anything I can do for you, Mistuh Paddock?"

Paddock returned her cheerful grin. Susan was loud, profane, sometimes obscene and with no more morals than an alley cat. She entertained soldiers in her cabin at night, both black soldiers and white. Paddock said, "Save me a pie, Susan. Apple."

"Good as done, Mistuh Paddock. You all goin' out with them soldiers after the Indians?"

He nodded.

"You watch your step, Mistuh Paddock. Them Indians remind me of a big ole cat playin' with a mouse. Standin' out there all day yellin', callin' the soldiers sonsabitches an' tellin' 'em to come out an' fight."

"I'll watch my step." He went on and came around the corner of the cavalry stables. He now could see the entire parade and the assembled troops. Susan had only echoed his own doubts about the sortie today but he knew that once having spoken his mind, there was nothing further he could do. Carrington had been painfully aware of the criticism among his junior officers of his failure to take the field against the Sioux. He had stubbornly resisted their demands as long as the necessary buildings within the fort's stockade were incomplete. Now he was acceding to them but Paddock suspected he was doing so unwillingly and against his better judgment.

Even now, Paddock could hear an Indian yelling outside the stockade. He walked to it and climbed to the banquette. The Indian was standing on the far side of Little Piney Creek, half hidden by high grass and brush. Paddock grinned because it was strange to hear an Indian speak English with a British accent. The Sioux must have learned his English from a Britisher, perhaps at one of the posts of the Hudson's Bay Company.

He climbed down, thinking that only the fort's artillery kept the Indians at a respectful distance. They feared it and knew what havoc it could cause with its cannister shot.

Among the infantry Lt. Grummond had assembled, he spotted O'Mara's burly figure and unruly shock of reddish hair. He walked toward the line of troopers, his eyes steadily on O'Mara's face.

O'Mara saw him and scowled. Lt. Grummond dismissed the troopers, after telling them to be ready to assemble with horses and full combat equipment at a moment's notice.

Paddock intercepted O'Mara. He extended the knife to the sergeant, handle first. "I believe this is yours."

O'Mara took it without batting an eye. "I take it you didn't rat on me or I'd be in the guardhouse."

"What happened was between you and me."

O'Mara growled, "It ain't over, Bucko. You cheated me last night."

In the same conversational tone, Paddock said, "You know you can say that out here and get away with it. But you're a lying sonofabitch and a bushwhacker as well. Keep away from me. Next time you won't get off as easy as you did last night."

O'Mara's scowl deepened at the words. He turned and tramped toward the stables to saddle up a horse.

Paddock heard a voice at his elbow, recognizing it immediately as that of Lt. Grummond. "What was that all about?"

"Nothing, Lieutenant. A personal matter."

"Don't let it interfere."

"It won't."

Grummond hesitated. "You're going out with Colonel Carrington and me, aren't you?"

Paddock nodded.

"So is O'Mara. If he was the one in your room last night, I'd advise you to keep him in front of you."

Paddock liked the lieutenant and it showed in the way he met Grummond's glance. "I'll remember that, Lieutenant."

"Get your horse saddled. There is no way of telling when the attack on the wood detail will come."

"I'll be ready." He watched the lieutenant walk across the parade toward his quarters, then turned and headed for the stables to get his horse.

Paddock had two horses stabled here at Fort Phil Kearny. His riding horse was a sorrel, deepchested and longlegged, an animal that could outrun and outlast the best owned by the Sioux.

The other was a brown mare he used as a pack animal. He caught the sorrel out of the corral, led him to the stables and saddled him. He left the cinch loose and hung the bridle over the saddle horn, leaving the halter on. He gave the animal a couple of forks of hay. Leaving the stables, he walked to the stockade and climbed up onto the banquette so that he could look over the top.

The wood detail was out of sight behind a knoll about a mile and a half from the fort. No Indians were in sight.

He stared moodily at the landscape. Snow covered most of it, except for the south-facing slopes, some of which were now bare in spots.

Phil Kearny was backed up against Little Piney Creek just west of the junction of the two branches of the creek. The Bozeman Road ran south to north immediately west of the fort. It skirted the eastward end of the Sullivant Hills, skirted Lodge Trail Ridge on the east, climbed an unnamed bluff and descended into Peno Creek beyond. It was visible from the fort almost to the point where it climbed the unnamed bluff.

Death was commonplace, both at Fort Phil Kearny and along the Bozeman Trail. Hardly a wagon train reached the fort that had not been attacked by Indians. Hardly a party of travelers journeyed north along the Bozeman Trail who did not have to fight somewhere along the way. The Sioux had not attacked the fort itself, and probably would not, due to their fear of artillery. But they would attack everything else that moved.

Uneasiness stirred in Paddock's mind. He smelled a trap in the way the Indians attacked the wood details with such a monotonous sameness every day. He smelled a trap in the way they always withdrew the minute a relief force came in sight.

They always retreated along the same route, which, to Paddock, also suggested a trap. And if the cavalry did not pursue, they invariably halted and shouted taunts, in an attempt to draw them on.

Shaking his head, he got down and walked across the parade. The troops had been dismissed and had gone to their quarters. A few stood on the banquette staring in the direction the wood train had gone.

At eight, the sentries on the stockade were changed. The Corporal of the Guard marched his relief detail around the fort's perimeter. It was a sloppy, straggling performance. Glancing across the parade Paddock saw Fetterman and Brown watching, disgust evident in the way they stood.

Paddock let his glance rest curiously on Brown. The captain wore one revolver holstered in the customary manner on his right side. He wore a second thrust into his belt. Spurs dangled from the buttonholes of his coat. His hat was tilted rakishly. He stood with legs spread, trunk and head thrust forward aggressively.

Paddock had heard him say that he wanted to kill an Indian before he was transferred to Fort Laramie. Kill an Indian. *Any* Indian. He had been heard to say he preferred Red Cloud, but he wasn't going back without a scalp.

A murderous attitude for a regular army

officer, Paddock thought. But it was only a manifestation of an attitude all too prevalent on the frontier — that Indians were not human. They were only some kind of wild prairie animal, whose pelts were to be sought as souvenirs.

Brown and Fetterman were two of a kind. Fetterman claimed he could ride through the whole Sioux nation with a hundred mounted men.

Shrugging lightly, Paddock headed for the sutler's store. Suddenly he wanted a drink. And suddenly he had the uneasy feeling that he should not go out with Carrington today.

At one o'clock, the picket on Pilot Hill, a mile and a half south of the fort, fired three rapid shots. At almost the same instant, one of the sentries shouted that a messenger was approaching from the direction of the Pinery.

The ponderous gates swung back, and the excited messenger, a private in H Company, rode through.

Carrington, Fetterman, Brown and several other officers had come from their quarters and stood at the edge of the parade looking toward the gates. Jess Paddock came from the sutler's store, a half-smoked cigar clamped between his teeth.

The messenger galloped across the parade and dismounted in front of the group of officers. He saluted and his words were clearly audible to Paddock all the way across the silent parade. "Indians have attacked the wood detail, sir. We were on our way back with our load of logs when . . ."

Paddock didn't hear the rest. A bugle called and men began pouring from the barracks at both ends of the parade. They ran toward the stables, and disappeared inside.

Paddock hurried past the guardhouse, also headed for the stables. He saw Molly Benedict come from her cabin, soapsuds to her elbows. She raised a hand to shield her eyes from the glare of the sky and he waved at her. Then he hurried on.

He collided with a man coming out of the stables, leading his horse at a run. He could hear firing now from the direction of the Pinery. The wagons of the wood train had undoubtedly been drawn into a hollow square. The men were fighting the Indians from beneath and behind them as they usually did.

The stable was a shambles, but he shouldered his way to the stall where he had left his horse. Quickly he exchanged the halter for the bridle and cinched the saddle down. He led the horse outside, mounted and trotted him to his quarters in the quarter-master corral. He went inside, got his rifle and revolver and came back out again.

The men were assembling raggedly on the parade. Nobody seemed to be making any effort to make them draw up into some kind of military formation.

Paddock spotted Col. Carrington and rode to him. The colonel was talking to Fetterman. "Go ahead, Colonel Fetterman. Relieve the wood train and pursue the Indians when they retreat."

Fetterman nodded. His face was pale and taut. There was excitement in his eyes. He galloped toward the gate, waving his men on with a forward flung right arm. Lt. Bingham shouted excitedly, "Fo'ward, ho!"

The two dozen or so cavalrymen galloped after him, looking more like a mob of civilians than a detachment of cavalry. They thundered through the gates, which closed ponderously behind them.

Paddock sat his horse, waiting, while Col. Carrington looked over his mounted infantrymen. The feeling of uneasiness he had experienced earlier returned. It was as if he knew something was going to happen to him out there today. He shook the thought off irritably.

CHAPTER 4

From the back of his horse Paddock could see over the log stockade. He could see the wood road, stretching away emptily until it disappeared behind the knoll.

Captain Brown, in his unholy eagerness to kill an Indian, had not waited for Fetterman, Bingham and the cavalry to leave the fort. Without authorization, he had taken two mounted infantrymen and had galloped away as soon as the messenger arrived to report the wood train under attack. He and the two enlisted men were now nearly a mile from the fort, ahead of Fetterman and the cavalry by more than half a mile. As Paddock watched, they left the road and climbed the western slope of the Sullivant Hills to get a view of the besieged wood train beyond the knoll that hid it from the fort. They halted halfway up the slope and stared toward the west for several minutes. Then they charged their horses recklessly down the slope, taking the road again slightly ahead of Fetterman and the cavalry.

Colonel Carrington shouted, "Open the gates!"

The gates swung open. Carrington said, "Ride with me, Jess. You too, Lieutenant Grummond."

The three cantered out through the gate with the force of mounted infantrymen straggling along behind, some at a canter, some at a trot.

There was a rise between the two forks of Piney Creek, a kind of low ridge which was an extension of the Sullivant Hills. Cresting it, Paddock could see the wood train drawn up in a hollow square. The Indians were retreating, and Fetterman's force of cavalry was approaching at a full gallop. Between the wood train and the fort, Paddock could see another man galloping, rifle in hand. It looked like Wands but he could not be sure.

So far everything seemed to be proceeding according to plan in spite of the undisciplined excitement of both officers and enlisted men. Glancing behind, Paddock saw O'Mara staring at him malevolently, and he reminded himself that when the shooting started he had better keep O'Mara in front of him if possible.

Fetterman and the cavalry caught up with Brown and the two mounted infantrymen and left the road, pursuing the retreating Indians up over the Sullivant Hills along the escape route they always used. The wood train left its corralled position and continued once more toward the fort, traveling in two parallel columns as they always did so that forming the protective square would be quicker and easier.

Ahead of Paddock, Carrington and Lt. Grummond began to descend into the valley of Big Piney Creek, heading for the Bozeman Road crossing. There was a flurry of firing from Fetterman's direction, the reports sounding like exploding firecrackers.

They reached the crossing. Ice had formed on the water and it was impossible to tell how thick it was. Colonel Carrington tried to force his horse out onto it, but the horse balked, plunging and fighting for his head. Carrington cursed irritably and raked the animal with his spurs. Fighting, plunging, the horse finally took to the ice and promptly went to his haunches as his hind feet slipped and went out from under him.

Paddock grinned. Carrington, for all his age and dignity, rode the horse like a cowboy riding a bucking bronc. He forced the horse, foot by foot, out onto the thin

success. Their big cavalry horses were apparently winded by the long gallop from the fort while the small, wiry ponies of the Sioux were comparatively fresh.

It was an old and familiar story. The Sioux only fought when they wanted to and they never fought unless the odds were overwhelmingly in their favor. They'd elude Fetterman easily unless Carrington's force cut them off.

Carrington waved an arm and the command moved back to the right so that they would be hidden by the crest of the ridge. Nearly a mile ahead half a dozen Sioux pickets were retreating in front of them. All but three disappeared. The three stationed themselves on the highest point of the ridge, from there watching the troops advance.

Reaching a high point on the north edge of the ridge some minutes later, Paddock looked down and saw a bunch of Indians hidden in a deep ravine. He pointed them out to Carrington who counted them aloud. Thirty-two. They were apparently waiting for Fetterman's command to pass below them. Plainly visible on the Bozeman Road to the right of the ravine were four pickets.

There was now a look of concern on

Carrington's face. He was shivering visibly and his teeth were chattering from the cold. Standing in his stirrups, he waved his little command forward, spurring and forcing his horse to a gallop now. They thundered up the crest of the ridge toward the high point where the Indian pickets were, now perhaps half a mile away. Ahead, like quail flushed from underbrush, Indians came out of hiding and retreated, just out of effective rifle range.

Paddock realized that Carrington was afraid that Fetterman, in his eagerness, might get ahead of him, thus spoiling the plan worked out the night before. Reaching the high point from which the three Sioux pickets had retreated, they could look down into the valley of the west fork of Peno Creek. Several groups of Indians were galloping toward the east, closely followed by Fetterman's troop of cavalry. They were, perhaps, a mile away.

It was impossible to count the enemy at this distance, but Paddock's estimate ranged from a hundred to a hundred and fifty. To see Fetterman chasing that many Indians was a good bit like watching a mouse chasing a cat and Paddock couldn't help smiling to himself. Carrington's command had halted for a moment to let the horses blow.

Gunfire suddenly erupted in the valley as the Indians stopped running and turned to fight. From ravines to north and south, other small groups of Indians poured, to reinforce those already on the valley floor.

Carrington stood in his stirrups and waved an arm, shouting, "Forward! Ho!" Immediately he forced his horse to gallop, despite the scattered timber, brush and occasional rocks upon the slope. Lt. Grummond dropped back, ranging along the line of galloping troopers to see that none of them fell behind. Paddock kept pace with the Colonel, who, in the hope of letting Fetterman know he was coming, drew his service revolver and fired a couple of shots into the air.

The shots may or may not have been heard by Fetterman but some of the Indians turned their heads to look at this unexpected force galloping toward them from their flank. Uncertain, perhaps, as to how large a force it really was and suspecting they could see only part of it, they retreated toward the east, breaking off the engagement with Fetterman.

Fetterman's cavalry immediately pursued them on across the valley of the west fork of Peno Creek and, once more fearing Fetterman's cavalry might get ahead of him and thus spoil the plan, Carrington turned and headed across a saddle toward the east fork of Peno Creek, obviously intending to descend into it and follow it north to the point where it flowed into Peno Creek.

To Paddock he shouted, "Stay here, Jess, and watch which way Fetterman goes. I think they'll lead him down into Peno Creek, and if they do, I'll be to their rear."

Paddock nodded and angled his horse away from the galloping command. He caught a glimpse of Sergeant O'Mara's face as the man thundered past and he thought the sergeant looked disappointed at seeing him stay behind.

As for himself, he was relieved, because he'd been able to figure no way he could keep O'Mara in front of him when the shooting began. Fascinated, he watched the battle going on below.

The Indians, more than a hundred strong, had now all but surrounded Fetterman's little force of cavalry. Ringing in a horseshoe formation, they were closing in.

Fetterman's men were still moving stubbornly forward and as they did, the horseshoe of Indians retreated toward the east. But instead of turning north down the valley of the west fork, they retreated toward the top of a low ridge dividing the two tributaries and halfway up forced Fetterman and his men to stop.

Still uncertain as to which way Fetterman would finally go, Paddock remained watching. The pressure from the Indian horseshoe increased. Arrows rained among Fetterman's cavalry. Gunfire, ragged and undisciplined, crackled on the little ridge. Fetterman's cavalry began to give way, to retreat, despite the shouted and angry exhortations of their officers to stand fast and stop the Indian advance. Paddock could see Fetterman standing in his stirrups, waving his revolver, shouting angrily at his men.

Suddenly and unexpectedly, about half of the force of cavalry broke away from the others and galloped toward the rear, out of the open end of the horseshoe that was closing so fast. Paddock could hear the shouts of Fetterman faintly, but the fleeing cavalrymen did not heed.

It was not an ordered retreat; it was a rout. It was panic, outright cowardice, and it left the remaining cavalrymen at the mercy of the surrounding Indians. Appalled, Paddock watched as the fleeing troopers, led by Lt. Bingham, managed their escape from the horseshoe, then turned and veered east toward where Paddock sat his horse, toward the place they had seen Carrington only a few minutes earlier.

Seeing half their enemy fleeing, the Indians suddenly began to scream fiercely and redoubled their efforts to panic the remaining cavalrymen. Recklessly they rode in closer, to a range where their arrows and lances would be more accurate.

Fetterman, Brown, and Wands ordered the remaining men to dismount and coolly waited for the Sioux to reach point-black range. When the Indians did, a murderous volley crackled and half a dozen Indians fell. A second volley killed three or four more. After that, Lt. Wands' repeating rifle brought down at least one more. Shocked at their sudden losses, the Indians precipitantly drew back out of range.

Paddock had seen enough. Carrington would want to know about this development as soon as possible: he would immediately change his plan of battle and ride to Fetterman's relief.

Bingham and the fleeing cavalrymen were less than half a mile away as Paddock put his horse into a gallop, descended into the west fork and thundered up the ridge beyond along the trail left by Carrington and his men. Glancing to his left, he saw Lt. Bingham's white and frightened face. Bingham turned to follow him, understanding, perhaps, that Paddock would lead him to Carrington.

Bingham and his men were galloping their horses recklessly; but now, instead of heading straight toward Paddock, they were angling toward what appeared to be his destination, a small spur between two upper branches of the east fork of Peno Creek. It appeared to Paddock that they would reach the spot at about the same time he did, or perhaps a little ahead of him.

Bingham's army career was at an end. If he wasn't court-martialed for cowardice, he would at least be forced to resign.

But Paddock knew what had happened was the natural and inevitable consequence of leading untrained recruits into battle against an overwhelmingly superior force. Probably two-thirds of the men involved in this action today had never fired at another man, nor been fired upon before.

Paddock's premonition of the night before seemed now to have been justified. But he got no satisfaction out of being right. He only hoped Carrington and his men could get back to Fetterman before it was too late.

CHAPTER 5

There was a pocket of timber halfway up the slope of the saddle that separated the two forks of north Peno Creek. Bingham and his defecting cavalrymen were about a quarter mile west and riding as if the devil were in pursuit.

Suddenly, out of the timber ahead of Paddock, half a dozen Indians rode. They spotted him and immediately changed their heading and came galloping toward him.

Paddock veered east, sinking his spurs into his horse's sides. The surprised animal immediately began to run, and Paddock raked him again with the spurs, leaning low over his withers as the Indians, now less than a hundred yards away, began loosing their arrows at him.

The range was too great for accuracy, and few of the arrows reached him. The Indians began slowly to fall behind. As they did, Paddock circled gradually back toward the north so that he could rejoin Carrington. He had no wish to be caught out here alone by any large body of Indians. Cut off, his guns would be of little use before he was overwhelmed by the Sioux.

Reaching a high point of land, he could see Carrington's command ahead, strung out, with the stragglers almost a quarter mile behind the main body of the command. Carrington now encountered the group of men who had deserted Fetterman with Lt. Bingham, and who had gotten ahead of him. He passed them and went on.

Bingham's defecting cavalry seemed to be demoralized. They had dismounted and were huddled together in a shallow ravine, their horses held so that they served as a bulwark against attack. Paddock had seen Carrington wave an arm and shout, ordering the men to mount and follow him, but they had not obeyed. They remained in the ravine. Bingham was nowhere in sight.

Paddock experienced a sudden and disquieting uneasiness. The way Carrington's men were strung out, they were extremely vulnerable to a flanking attack if any large body of Indians happened to be in the vicinity. The dismounted and demoralized cavalrymen were also vulnerable, having no officer to rally them and tell them what to do.

Paddock spurred his horse again. He

could see up the long slope leading east. He spotted Lt. Bingham and Lt. Grummond now, together with three enlisted men, galloping their mounts through the scattered timber that covered the ridge, hotly pursuing about thirty Indians.

One Indian's horse lagged and Bingham leveled his revolver and fired at him. Paddock could see the puff of powdersmoke. The horse went to his knees and then collapsed. The Indian, thrown clear, scrambled to his feet and fled up the slope afoot.

Bingham galloped after him excitedly. He leveled his pistol again but this time no smoke billowed from its muzzle. Bingham threw it away disgustedly and drew his sword, afterward cutting viciously at the fleeing Sioux with it whenever he drew close enough.

The remaining Indians, reinforced by others who had ridden over the ridge from the east, now stopped, turned and charged back down toward Grummond and the others. Grummond and the enlisted men, seeing that they would be overrun, veered left along the side of the slope.

For some reason Lt. Bingham did not follow the other four. He rode straight into the oncoming wave of Indians, savagely cutting at them with his sword. He was almost immediately surrounded and overwhelmed. He disappeared from the back of his horse into the milling group of Indians.

Paddock felt a chill run along his spine. He knew what Bingham's fate would be. He was doomed and if he was allowed to die quickly he would be a lucky man. His body, when it was found, would be filled with arrows shot into it after it was stripped, and it would be mutilated beyond belief. The Sioux knew how to hate. The white man's fort was a cancer they could not cut away because of the white man's artillery. So their hatred showed itself whenever they managed to catch a white man helpless and alone.

But Bingham's inner torment prior to death must have been worse than anything the Sioux could do to him. A military man, he had turned and run from the enemy. He had abandoned comrades to what he believed to be certain death. Worse, he had led inexperienced recruits in a humiliating rout when he should have given them an example of courage and steadiness.

His self-hatred must have been intolerable. And when from the bottom of the shallow ravine, he had seen Carrington, Grummond and the others approaching, he must have grasped desperately at the fleeting chance to redeem himself. Recklessly he had called to Grummond and three enlisted men to follow him, and had charged toward the Bozeman Road in pursuit of twenty-five or thirty Indians threatening Carrington's flank.

There was no time for Paddock to further consider Lt. Bingham's fate. Carrington was still trying to reach the valley of Peno Creek ahead of Fetterman, whom he still believed was pursuing fleeing Indians down its course. Paddock could see Carrington's stragglers ahead, and looked for O'Mara specifically, without being able to pick him out.

Galloping, he passed the huddled cavalrymen. To them he roared, "Lieutenant Bingham's dead. You will be too if you don't follow me!"

He didn't wait to see if they would comply or not. He thundered away in the direction Carrington had gone. He wondered whether Fetterman's force had been overrun and he wondered what was ahead of Carrington.

He pounded past a group of a dozen or so stragglers from Carrington's command. He shouted, "For God's sake, close up!" as he heard firing ahead. He knew what these men did not, that Fetterman was pinned down by over a hundred Indians, that there could be as many as a hundred engaging Carrington and the few who had kept up with him.

Coming out of a scattering of timber, Paddock glimpsed Carrington and half a dozen men ahead. They had reached a bend from which point they could look down into the valley of Peno Creek. Not seeing Fetterman, the colonel had turned and looked back uncertainly in the direction he had come. He saw Paddock galloping toward him. At the same instant, between fifty and a hundred Indians charged him from the slope on his left. Their arrows literally filled the air, some falling short, some falling in the midst of the pitifully small body of men.

Paddock saw O'Mara with this group. Private McGuire fell with his horse on top of him. An Indian galloped in, knife in hand, to finish him and secure his scalp. Carrington roared an order at his men to dismount and fight on foot. Kneeling, he himself knocked the scalp-hungry Indian from his horse with a single shot.

The Indians charged again. Paddock reached Carrington's little group while the screaming horde was less than a hundred yards away. Carrington shouted, "Hold your fire! Wait until you can empty a saddle with every shot!"

At fifty feet, the troopers' ragged volley rolled out and three Indians were driven from their horses' backs. The rest, screaming furiously, veered away, after loosing their arrows at the soldiers kneeling on the ground.

In the lull following, Paddock shouted at Carrington, "Fetterman is pinned down back there, Colonel, and half his men have deserted him! He won't be coming down Peno Creek!"

He could see in Carrington a sudden fear that this sortie against the Sioux was about to turn into a major disaster. His command was widely scattered and surrounded by howling, bloodthirsty Indians that outnumbered them ten to one. If he did not quickly regroup his forces, disaster was inevitable.

Carrington glanced around, worried but not panicking. He stared at the high ground on the right, at the ridge along which ran the Bozeman Road. It offered not only a commanding height, but an easy route back to the fort. He shouted, "Prepare to mount!" and almost immediately afterward, "Mount!"

The troopers swung to their saddles.

Carrington waved an arm toward the ridge on the right. "Forward! Ho!"

He led the men across the shallow valley and began the ascent through scattered timber toward the crest of the ridge. To Paddock he shouted, "Go back and bring the stragglers! O'Mara, go with him!"

Paddock held his horse still a few moments, giving O'Mara time to reach him. O'Mara scowled briefly but the situation was too desperate for personal animosity and the scowl did not remain. Side by side the pair galloped up the ravine, yelling at the stragglers to close up, to bear right and rejoin the colonel on the slope.

One group of about a dozen men galloped their horses and rejoined Carrington before he and his men had much more than started up the slope. The Indians, readying themselves for another charge, changed their minds when they saw Carrington's group strengthened. Howling their disappointment, they retreated eastward down the valley of Peno Creek.

Paddock and O'Mara located the last of the stragglers and, shortly afterward, the group of cavalrymen who had deserted Fetterman. Both shouted at the men to get on up the ridge and join Carrington. The men, galvanized at last by specific orders, mounted their horses and galloped them up the slope toward Carrington's men.

Paddock said, "I'm going to find Fetterman."

O'Mara nodded, saying, "And I'm going to see that those bastards get where they're going this time." He spurred away and followed the group of cavalrymen.

Paddock swung his horse westward, now climbing the ridge that separated the two forks of the narrow creek. At the top, he encountered Fetterman with about a dozen men. The man looked harassed and worried. When he saw Paddock, he shouted, "Where's Carrington?"

Paddock pointed toward his rear, "He wants you to join him at the top of that ridge."

In a more normal tone of voice Fetterman asked, "Where's Bingham, and where are the men he had with him?"

"Bingham's dead. The men he had with him are all right. Last I saw of them they were heading up that slope with Sergeant O'Mara herding them along."

"How was Bingham killed?"

Fetterman now was riding at Paddock's side. Both men held their horses to a steady trot. The cavalrymen followed along, occasionally glancing worriedly toward the rear. They'd had about all the fighting they wanted for today, Paddock thought. Even Fetterman seemed subdued.

Paddock said, "Colonel, Bingham panicked and I guess he was sorry afterward. He tried to redeem himself. He and Lieutenant Grummond and three men charged up that slope into about thirty or forty Indians, to protect Colonel Carrington's flank. When more Indians came over the ridge, Grummond and the three men went back down but Bingham charged right on up into the middle of them."

"Has his body been found?"

"Nobody's had time to look for it, Colonel. But I don't guess it'll be very hard to find."

Fetterman said, "If he'd stood fast, we'd have been all right."

Paddock didn't answer. But he was thinking that Bingham's panic hadn't been entirely his fault. He had simply been too green to cope with full-scale combat.

CHAPTER 6

Fetterman's little force straggled up the slope to join Carrington at the top of the ridge. The wagon ruts of the Bozeman Road were visible in places where the snow had melted or blown away. Carrington, until being told by Fetterman, had not known that Lt. Bingham was dead. Now, he ordered the men to spread out and move eastward to search for the lieutenant's body.

The command had no sooner left the crest of the ridge when Lt. Grummond and two of the three who had been with him came galloping up out of a timbered ravine.

Grummond was flushed and his eyes were narrowed with anger. He rode to Col. Carrington and halted in front of him. His words were loud and intemperate as he furiously asked Carrington whether he was a fool or a coward for failing to come to his and Lt. Bingham's aid.

Paddock didn't hear Carrington's reply, because his voice was not as loud as Lt.

Grummond's had been. He was surprised that Carrington bothered to answer at all. Most commanding officers, addressed that way by a subordinate, would have immediately placed the offending subordinate under arrest.

Paddock was beginning to feel considerable sympathy for Carrington. The man had mounted this offensive against his better judgment because of pressure from his junior officers. His reluctance to take the field against overwhelmingly superior numbers and with untrained recruits had been vindicated by the happenings today. Yet now he was being accused of cowardice, or at the very least of being stupid when the real blame rested on Lt. Bingham's foolish compulsion to redeem himself. Carrington hadn't even seen what happened, either to Bingham or to Grummond and the other three.

Jess Paddock rode his horse to the two officers. He was as angry as Lt. Grummond was, but in him it only showed as narrowed eyes and a mouth that was compressed. He said thinly, "Lieutenant, you and Bingham left the colonel's command without his knowledge and without orders. I saw what happened to you but the colonel did not. How could he possibly ride to your rescue when he didn't even know you were in trouble? If there is a fool here today, I would say that it was you."

Grummond's face turned an even deeper red. For several moments he was too furious to speak. Before he could, Carrington interrupted, his normally even voice touched with anger at last. "That will be all, gentlemen! We are out here to fight Indians, not to argue among ourselves. Lieutenant Grummond, rejoin your men!"

Scowling, Grummond turned his horse and rode away. He returned almost immediately. "Sergeant Bower is back there, sir, with an arrow in him and with his skull split open by a tomahawk." His tone of voice was accusatory, as if Carrington was personally responsible.

Carrington said sharply, "Then take some men and get back to him. Don't leave him lying there." He turned to Paddock. "Ride back to the fort, Jess, and have an ambulance sent out — with a sufficient escort to protect it from attack."

Paddock nodded. "Right, Colonel." He whirled his horse and galloped away toward the fort.

Riding along the road, the going was easy and he made good time. He covered the four miles in less than half an hour.

The gates swung open as he approached. Brevet Major Powell, commanding in Col. Carrington's absence, met him just inside the gate. "What happened, Jess?"

"Long story, Major. But Lieutenant Bingham is dead and Sergeant Bower probably is too. The colonel wants an ambulance sent out, along with a large enough escort to protect it from attack."

"Where is the colonel now?"

"Four miles north on the Bozeman Road."

Powell turned and spoke to a private, who immediately turned and sprinted across the parade toward the stables. Paddock said, "I'm going back, Major. Any message for Colonel Carrington?"

"Just that the ambulance is on its way."

Paddock turned his horse and rode back toward the north. He knew he should have taken time to get a fresh horse. But he'd been afraid that if he did, he'd be ordered to accompany the ambulance.

When he reached the place he'd left Carrington, he found about a dozen men squatting in a clump of trees. Bower's body lay nearby, covered with a tarpaulin. Paddock asked a corporal, "Where is Colonel Carrington?"

The man gestured toward the east. "Still huntin' fer Lieutenant Bingham over on that ridge."

Paddock nodded and took the descending slope leading toward the east. He could see a thin line of blue-clad troopers about a mile away, working their way up toward the top of a low ridge.

His horse was covered with sweat despite the chill. He wondered suddenly how Carrington had stood it, being out here in the cold, soaking wet all afternoon. But Carrington hadn't said a word about being uncomfortable.

He caught up with the line of troopers just as one of them shouted, "Colonel! Here he is!"

Immediately, all the troopers rode toward the sound. Paddock reached there slightly ahead of Carrington. Half a dozen troopers were gathered in a circle around the body, staring down, their faces pale with shock.

The body lay face down over a dead and rotted stump surrounded by heavy brush. It had been stripped naked and from it protruded over fifty arrows. Some of them must have been shot into him before his death, because blood had trickled from the wounds. Others had apparently been shot into him after death, in a frenzy of hatred and excitement.

Paddock glanced at Colonel Carrington. The man's face was white and his eyes were narrowed with pain that seemed almost physical. He said, "Wrap him in blankets and load him on a horse. Let's get back to the top of the ridge."

Wrapping Bingham's body in blankets with that many arrows sticking into him was difficult, but the men managed it. They tied the blankets in place by winding rope around the lieutenant's body. Four of them hoisted him across the saddle of a horse and tied him down. The little cavalcade headed west toward the Bozeman Road on the spine of the ridge.

As they crested the slope and rode out of the timber, Paddock heard the creak of wagon wheels and saw the ambulance approaching from the direction of the fort.

The vehicle turned around and the bodies of Bower and Bingham were loaded into it. The wounded also were permitted to ride. Saddles and gear from horses that had been killed were loaded into the ambulance with them. The command headed back toward the fort. The sun had already set and it was getting dark.

It was a grim column of soldiers that filed back down the road toward the fort.

The expedition against the Indians had been a dismal failure. A few Indians had been killed, but not enough so that the survivors would feel defeated or even chastised. Worse, the Sioux had seen the United States Army break and run, and the knowledge that they could force the white soldiers to turn tail would make them even more arrogant than they had been before.

It was almost seven o'clock before the straggling command reached the fort. The gates swung open. First through was Colonel Carrington, followed by Paddock, Brown and Fetterman. The ambulance came next and behind the ambulance came Dr. Hines, followed by Lieutenants Grummond and Wands.

The ambulance turned immediately after entering the gate and headed straight for the post hospital. There was no attempt made to draw the command into line for proper dismissal. The men simply scattered once they were through the gate, each to take care of his own horse and then to head for his barracks mess for supper.

Paddock suddenly realized how tired he was. Surprisingly, he glimpsed a white and familiar face among those lined up on both sides of the gate and immediately rode to her. He dismounted, startled at her intensity as Molly ran to him and threw her arms around his neck.

She hugged him hard for a moment and when she finally drew back she left his cheek wet with her tears. Jess said, "Here! Here! There's nothing to cry about!"

"Nothing to cry about? You've been out there six hours and we've heard shooting all that time and no word sent back to the post and you say there's nothing to cry about?"

Jess grinned and gathered her into his arms again. He held her tightly until she stopped crying. Then, with an arm around her he walked her across the cold and wind-swept parade toward the beckoning lights beyond. He said, "I could eat a horse."

"I've got some Irish stew."

"Sounds good." He squeezed her appreciatively.

There was noise already coming from the sutler's store, as the men who had money began celebrating their safe return.

Paddock saw Carrington give his horse to an enlisted man and then walk toward his quarters across the dark parade. Against the snow that covered the parade, he made a slumped and dejected silhouette.

Paddock watched until the door of his quarters closed after him.

Molly was silent all the way to her door. There was a lamp burning inside and the room was warm. The delicious smell of stew and of coffee filled the air. She found a bottle of whisky and a glass and brought them to him. He grinned. "You're just going to have to marry me, Molly Benedict."

She poured him a stiff drink and corked the bottle, "You're just hungry now."

He shook his head. "I mean it. I want to take you back to Fort Laramie with the next escort that heads out of here." He was remembering the premonition he'd had this morning, the uneasiness he'd felt last night.

She was studying him, her face still pale, her eyes concerned. "Something's the matter. What is it?"

He said, "That was a disaster out there today. It's a miracle the whole command wasn't wiped out to a man. Worst of all, Lieutenant Bingham and about a dozen men ran, and now that the Indians know they can make white soldiers run, they'll be more cocky than they ever were before."

"The colonel won't try anything like that again, will he? After the experience he had today?"

70

"I wouldn't bet on it. Brown is still breathing fire and Grummond is mad as a hornet because Carrington didn't come to his rescue when Lieutenant Bingham was killed."

"Why didn't the colonel rescue him?"

"He didn't even know Grummond and Bingham were under attack." He grinned ruefully. "As a matter of fact, they weren't. They were *chasing* the Indians. The Indians just stopped, turned around and began to chase *them* instead."

"Poor Lieutenant Bingham. He was so young."

Paddock nodded. "He was a good officer. All he needed was time and experience. He just lost his head. There must have been over a hundred screeching Indians around Bingham's cavalry and he'd never seen anything like that before. Then, after it was over, he was so ashamed that he tried to redeem himself by making a reckless attack on some Indians coming over the ridge from the east."

Molly shuddered. "Was it . . . was it quick?" she asked.

He nodded. "I saw him go down. It was quick all right."

She put a plate of stew in front of him and brought coffee immediately afterward.

He finished the whisky and began to eat. Molly said, "There won't be another escort going out of here for at least three weeks."

"Then you'll go with me?"

She nodded. "I'll go with you."

He got up, crossed the room and took her into his arms. Holding her, he admitted that he was still uneasy in spite of his decision to take Molly with him and leave.

He tried to put his doubts out of his mind. Molly had promised to marry him. They could put Fort Phil Kearny behind them. Jess had money enough to buy a good ranch in Kansas or Colorado Territory and enough to stock it.

They could raise a family . . . Then why did that damned core of uneasiness linger in the back of his mind?

CHAPTER 7

On the following morning the entire garrison of Fort Phil Kearny, and most of the civilians, assembled on the parade for funeral services. The bodies of Lieutenant Bingham and Sergeant Bower lay in flag-draped pine caskets, made during the night by the carpenters. The caskets had been placed side by side in an ambulance and the canvas sides rolled up to make them visible.

Carrington stood in the cold wind, which whipped his coat around his legs, and read as loudly as he could from the heavy Bible. After that, the regimental band played the Funeral March, and when the last notes had died away, Lt. Wands, in command of the burial detail, shouted, "Forward — Ho!"

Wands led out through the gate, followed by four troopers. The ambulance, drawn by a team of black mules, came next, and behind that rode the remainder of the escort. Behind the escort came another wagon, this one loaded with shovels, picks, black powder, and enough men to dig the graves quickly so that, with luck, the detail could be back in the fort before the Indians could mount an attack.

Jess Paddock rode behind the wagon. There was no particular reason for him to accompany this small detail but he wanted to ride to the top of Pilot Hill. He was curious as to what the Indians were doing and how many of them were still around.

The procession crossed Little Piney Creek and followed the two-track road to the cemetery. Paddock saw no Indians.

At the cemetery, Lt. Wands selected two gravesites and marked them out with his foot. He, the men of the escort, and the two wagons drew away and the workmen began to dig.

They first scraped snow and loose dirt from the graves. When they struck frozen ground, they brought star drills and sledges from the wagon and began to drill. They went down until they struck thawed ground and then poured black powder into the holes. Caps and fuses were next, and then earth to seal the holes. No more than one fuse was lighted at a time and there were eight in all. Each explosion made a dull thump and flung only a small geyser of dirt into the air. But afterward, the earth was cracked sufficiently so that the men could, with their picks, take out the fractured chunks.

Working swiftly in short shifts, the men had the two graves dug in less than an hour. Meanwhile Paddock had ridden his horse to the top of Pilot Hill. From there he stared out over the bleak winter landscape, at the near slopes of the Sullivant Hills, at the slope of Lodge Trail Ridge beyond, and along the Bozeman Road west of it. Still he saw no Indians.

They must be having a powwow, he thought, going over the happenings of yesterday in their councils, and planning what their next move would be.

The Sioux would be enormously elated. They had defeated the hated whites. They had routed Bingham and a dozen of his men. They had made Fetterman retreat and they had killed two white soldiers, one of them an officer.

They still might fear the fort's artillery. But no longer would they fear the men.

Paddock started down off Pilot Hill. The picket, standing atop the platform built for his use called, "Mr. Paddock?"

Jess turned his head. The man pointed to the northwest. Half a dozen mounted Sioux were sitting their horses on the top of Lodge Trail Ridge. They had just ridden into sight and were silhouetted against the sky.

Even at this great distance, he could make out their elaborate feathered head-dresses. Chiefs and Medicine Men, he thought. Red Cloud might be one of them.

Scarcely had he glimpsed the chiefs on the ridge when a rifle cracked below. Paddock immediately put his horse into a gallop down the side of Pilot Hill. Behind him, the picket cocked his weapon and stared around nervously.

Smoke had billowed out of some heavy brush about a hundred yards from the burial party. It had probably come from one of the muzzle-loading Springfields captured by the Indians yesterday, Paddock thought.

He reached the burial party. They were just now lowering the caskets into the graves by ropes, glancing over their shoulders nervously in the direction of the shot.

An arrow, arching high, came from the same direction and stuck in the canvas cover of the ambulance. Lt. Wands shouted, "Take cover behind the wagons!"

The men did so quickly. The caskets were already in the graves which a couple of men were filling, glancing fearfully every now and then toward the brush from which the shots had come.

Paddock reached Lt. Wands who was still sitting his horse. He said, "Give me half a dozen men, Lieutenant. There can't be more than two or three in there."

Wands nodded. Paddock said, "Anyone that wants to, come along."

Several men left the shelter of the wagons and ran for their horses. Paddock galloped toward the brush, the others following. He was almost instantly rewarded by seeing three Indians running ahead of him. They reached their horses, tied in the brush thirty or forty feet away, vaulted to their backs and thundered away. Paddock pulled his horse to a halt at about the spot from which the Indians had fired earlier. He yelled, "No use, boys!"

Turning, he trotted back to the burial party, the others following reluctantly. The graves were now almost filled. Three men were working on each one. Wands said, "I wonder how many guns they got yesterday."

"Check the men that went along. See if they all have theirs."

Wands chuckled shortly. "Those that lost their guns probably broke into the quartermaster storehouse last night and replaced them."

"I saw Bingham throw a pistol away. He

must have lost the other one earlier because he had been carrying two. And the Indians must have captured Bower's rifle when they killed him. They have those three at least."

The earth was now carefully mounded over the two fresh graves. One of the men took two white crosses from the wagon. On one was Lt. Bingham's name. On the other was that of Sgt. Bower. The man pushed them into the loose earth at the heads of the graves.

Lt. Wands shouted, "Let's go back." He rode toward the fort with Paddock riding at his side. The ambulance and wagon followed and the escort and workmen brought up the rear. There were no more shots and no Indians visible.

Halfway to the fort, Paddock asked, "Do you think Colonel Carrington will try going after the Indians again?"

Wands shrugged. Then he turned his head and grinned ruefully. "The pressure won't let up, that's sure. Brown and Fetterman haven't changed. Fetterman blames what happened on Carrington. He thinks that if Carrington had done what he was supposed to, everything would have turned out differently. And maybe so."

Paddock said, "I was with Carrington.

He was afraid Fetterman was going to get ahead of him. By the time the Indians stopped you, he couldn't see you any more. Besides that, he thought you were going to drive the Indians down the valley of Peno Creek. Instead, they came over the saddle between the two upper forks."

Lieutenant Wands shrugged. "It's over now. And hindsight is always a hell of a lot better than foresight, isn't it?"

The burial party entered the fort and Wands dismissed the men. Paddock headed for the stables. Even now, with the sun up, the wind was cold and raw. He wondered wryly if the wind ever stopped blowing here.

Nearing the stables, he heard someone call to him. Turning, he saw Lt. Grummond hurriedly crossing the parade.

Walking, leading his horse, Paddock turned back. He met Grummond near the magazine, a half buried building near the middle of the parade with a painted tin hip roof. Grummond said, "I want to talk to you."

Paddock nodded. "Talk away."

"What the hell was the big idea of jumping me in front of the colonel yesterday?"

Paddock moved away toward the bandstand in the center of the parade.

Grummond followed. Both men got out of the wind in the lee of the bandstand before Paddock answered. "Lieutenant, maybe I was out of line." Paddock liked Grummond and he didn't want to quarrel with him. He *had* been out of line in interfering between the commanding officer and a subordinate.

"You're damned right you got out of line." Grummond's face was red. He had come out here looking for a quarrel and he seemed balked by Paddock's refusal to enter into one.

He glared at Paddock a moment more. "I'll ask you to remember, mister, that you're only a *civilian.* You have no right. Stay out of things you don't understand."

Paddock felt his own temper stir. He said, "I understand well enough. I held the rank of major in the Confederate Army during the war. You were wrong, Lieutenant. Cut it any way you like, you still were wrong."

"Wrong? God damn it, he left us to shift for ourselves! We went up there to protect his flank and he left us to shift for ourselves!"

Paddock stared steadily at him, his eyes now smoldering. "Lieutenant, I hate to call a man a liar. But are you real damn sure that was what you and Bingham were trying to do? Bingham had just tucked his tail between his legs and run away. He must have been sick with shame. To make it worse, he went off and left the men who had run away with him. So he was out to redeem himself, no matter what he had to do to accomplish it. He didn't give a damn about Carrington's right flank. All he wanted was to prove to himself and to everybody else that he wasn't a coward, no matter what it took."

Grummond, his flush fading, asked, "What's so wrong with that? If you saw any action during the war you must know how he felt."

"I know."

"Then why condemn the man?"

"Hell, I'm not condemning him. I'm just saying that you had no more thought about Carrington's flank than Bingham did. You knew how Bingham felt and you wanted to help him vindicate himself. You took three enlisted men along and now one of them is dead."

All the color had faded from Grummond's face. "And you think Bower's death is my fault?"

"I'm not trying to blame anything on anyone. You're the one that laid it all on Carrington. You blamed him for Bingham's and Bower's death because he didn't come to your aid. But how the hell could he, when he didn't even know you were on that slope? There was timber between Carrington and you. I only saw you because I was over on the ridge opposite."

Grummond said savagely, "Damn it, Paddock —"

Paddock interrupted. "Lieutenant, Carrington was sent out here to build a fort. He's not a combat officer. Even so, I think he did pretty well yesterday. I was with him. Fetterman thinks he didn't do what he was supposed to, but Fetterman is wrong. The colonel was afraid Fetterman was going to get ahead of him and that would have been disastrous. Carrington kept bearing right to keep that from happening. It wasn't his fault the Indians retreated over the ridge between the two upper forks of Peno Creek instead of down the main valley the way they were supposed to. It wasn't his fault that Bingham took half Fetterman's men and ran away. That slowed Fetterman and ruined the whole plan."

Grummond glared at him. The wind was rising and even here in the lee of the bandstand it cut through and chilled both men.

There didn't seem to be much more to say. Paddock didn't want Grummond's

82

enmity. He said, "I'm sorry, Lieutenant. I don't want to quarrel with you."

"You should have thought of that yesterday." Grummond stared coldly at him for several moments. There was more he obviously wanted to say, but he didn't go on. Suddenly turning on his heel, he stalked away.

Paddock watched him go regretfully. Then, shrugging helplessly, he led his horse toward the stables across the snowcovered, wind-swept parade.

He was glad he was leaving soon. The dissension inside this isolated outpost could only worsen as time went on. There would be more instances of insubordination involving both officers and men. And if those instances occurred outside the stockade, they could easily turn out more disastrously than had the expedition yesterday.

They were a tiny nucleus of whites surrounded by thousands of hostile, warlike Sioux who wanted nothing more than to exterminate them all. One small mistake in judgment might be all it would take to give the Sioux their opportunity.

CHAPTER 8

Jess Paddock unsaddled his horse and put him into his stall. He gave him some hay, then stepped out into the cold wind again. Low clouds were scudding along overhead, their dark undersides brushing the crest of Lodge Trail Ridge. Paddock wondered if it was going to snow. It didn't feel like it, but the low clouds could be an indication of a new storm blowing in.

He hesitated for a moment in front of the stables, then turned and crossed the parade toward Col. Carrington's quarters on the western side. A steady hammering filled the air. Outside the fort, the sawmill screeched as the saw bit into a frozen log.

Paddock knocked on Carrington's door and was admitted by the colonel himself. He went in, quickly pulling the door closed behind him. The room was warm from a cast-iron potbellied stove. He removed his hat.

He said, "Colonel, I'm going to be leaving with the first escort that heads back to Fort Laramie."

Carrington frowned slightly. "I hope your decision has nothing to do with what happened yesterday."

Paddock shook his head. "It hasn't. Molly Benedict is going with me. We're going to be married."

Carrington's frown disappeared. He grinned and extended his hand. "Congratulations. Mrs. Benedict is a fine woman, indeed."

"I expect it'll be a couple of weeks before there will be an escort. In the meantime, Colonel, I'm available to help in any way I can."

Carrington nodded. "Good. I may want you to make a scout or two for me. I want no repetition of what happened yesterday." He studied Paddock narrowly. "How have *you* assessed our failure yesterday?"

Paddock grinned. "Simple, Colonel. Too many Indians."

"There was more to it than that."

"Yes sir. Green, untrained men. Inexperience. Failure to properly respect the capabilities of the Sioux."

"Fetterman thinks I let him down."

Paddock said, "You didn't let anybody down. You were trying to stay ahead of Fetterman so he wouldn't get ahead of you. Nobody could foresee that Bingham would take half of Fetterman's men and run away."

Carrington frowned. "I don't much like that way of describing it. He . . ."

"He vindicated himself?" Paddock suggested, shrugging. "At what cost, Colonel? Bower paid for Bingham's anxiety to redeem himself."

"Aren't you being a little hard on him? He paid with his own life too, you know."

"I know. And I'm not being hard on him. Not half as hard as he was on himself. He committed suicide, Colonel. You know it and I know it. And he took Bower along with him."

Carrington shuddered slightly. "Damned red-skinned barbarians! I wonder how long he lived after —"

"Not long, Colonel. Not more'n a minute or two."

"A minute or two can be a lifetime. I just wish I had a thousand men I could take out against them."

Paddock smiled wryly. "Don't blame the Indians too much, Colonel. They see us here and they know we're going to stay and that more will follow until they've been driven from their lands the way all the other tribes have."

Carrington said, "You like them, don't you, Jess?"

"Can't help it. I've known some of them. They really aren't barbarians, and they have a way of life a man can't help envying sometimes."

"Well, the fort is almost finished now and I'm going to start drilling the men every day. If it comes to a fight again, I want them to be more ready than they were yesterday."

Paddock nodded. "A good idea. But don't let the Indians draw you into anything against your will. They will also have learned something from what happened yesterday."

He opened the door and stepped quickly out into the bitter wind, closing it behind him as he did. Head down, he crossed the parade. As he went past the NCO quarters, someone yelled at him. He turned his head and saw O'Mara standing in the door.

A kind of wariness came to him. He felt it as tension in his arms and legs and in the way his heart speeded up. If O'Mara wanted a fight . . .

He approached the man and O'Mara called, "We're havin' a little game tonight, Bucko. We figure you owe us the chance to get our money back."

Paddock nodded. "I'll be there. Right after supper?"

O'Mara nodded. He was not scowling and there was a speculative quality about his glance. Paddock studied him curiously from a dozen feet away.

This was a different man from the one who had lost so heavily in the game day before yesterday. The action yesterday must have relaxed him, Paddock thought.

He turned back, and continued along the wind-swept street toward his quarters beyond in the quartermaster corral. He went in and immediately crossed to the stove and stirred the ashes, afterward adding a couple of sticks of firewood.

Frowning, he puzzled about the change in Sergeant O'Mara. He had credited the action yesterday with bringing about the change in the man, but was it really the fight that had been responsible? Wasn't it possible that O'Mara had rigged tonight's game so that he could win?

He shook his head. It didn't matter. If O'Mara wanted his money back badly enough to rig the game, then Paddock was willing to give it back.

He put O'Mara and the game resolutely out of his mind. He thought instead of Carrington and he couldn't help wondering if Carrington was going to let his junior officers push him into mounting another offensive against the Sioux. The colonel had wished aloud that he had a thousand men to lead against the Indians.

That was about what it would take to beat them, thought Paddock ruefully. A thousand seasoned men, and howitzers, repeating rifles instead of the single-shot Springfields with which most of the men were armed, and an unlimited quantity of ammunition. Only superior armament could overcome the numerical superiority of the Indians, who were, in addition, fighting for their homeland against an invader who, they knew, would take it all from them if he could.

Carrington obviously felt badly about the deaths of Bingham and Bower and he was smarting under Grummond's accusation of cowardice. Feeling as he did, he might be tempted to do something he ordinarily would not do.

Paddock stood close to the stove, trying to rid himself of the chill that lingered in his spine. He began to sweat beneath his heavy coat, but the chill did not go away. He removed his coat and began to pace angrily back and forth. He was getting to be a damned old woman, he told himself. He was making things up in his mind. Nothing was going to happen here at Fort

Phil Kearny. The stockade was strong, the howitzers ready day and night.

He stopped and stared out the streaked window. He glimpsed movement and saw Molly Benedict, with two buckets, walking along in the direction of the water gate. Grabbing his coat and shrugging into it, he hurried after her.

She wore her own heavy coat, its collar turned up against the biting wind. She had a scarf tied over her head. Paddock took the buckets out of her hands.

The wind was now so strong it snatched her words away. She caught his arm and they walked together, heads down, diagonally across the quartermaster corral to the water gate. There was a sentry at the gate which stood open enough to permit a person to pass through.

Paddock went through and filled the buckets in the stream. Rocks had been used to create a fill so that those wanting water could get it without wetting their feet. Carrying the buckets, Paddock came back through the gate. Molly asked, "Did you tell the Colonel that we were going to leave?"

He nodded.

"And?"

Paddock grinned. "He congratulated

me. Said you were a fine woman. A fine woman indeed is what he said. I think you have an admirer."

She did not answer him because by now they had left the shelter of the stockade and were exposed to the full sweep of the wind again.

Hurrying, they reached her tiny cabin. Colored Susan, just coming out of her own hut farther up the line, called with good-natured mockery, "Y'all kin carry water for me, Mistuh Paddock, if you through with hers."

"You're a big girl, Susan. Carry your own," he shouted back.

He put the buckets down inside while Molly closed the door. Turning, removing the scarf from her head, she asked, "Did the Colonel say when there would be an escort to Fort Laramie?"

Paddock shook his head. "He doesn't know. It will depend on when the supply train gets through to us. It's supposed to arrive before Christmas."

She nodded, her eyes studying him worriedly. He could see that the two deaths yesterday had disturbed her, frightened her. She said, "The time's so short. Nothing's going to happen, is it, Jess?"

He leaned down and kissed her lightly

on the nose. "Nothing's going to happen."

"Then get yourself out of here and let me do my work."

Paddock left, grinning to himself at her sudden change of tone.

At six-thirty, Paddock opened the door of the NCO quarters and stepped inside. The game was already in progress at a table about halfway between the two potbellied stoves. There were four men in the game and perhaps half a dozen onlookers.

Paddock took off his coat and laid it on a bench. He sat down opposite O'Mara. He knew what he was going to do but he doubted if even that would do any good. Furthermore, he wasn't sure how much he could lose to O'Mara without letting the sergeant and the other players know he was doing it deliberately. If O'Mara so much as suspected he was losing on purpose it would be worse than if he won.

O'Mara's face was already flushed from the excitement of the game. Paddock put his money on the table in front of him. Part of it consisted of well-worn greenbacks and yellowbacks, part of it gold coin. The four finished the hand they had been playing and the deal passed to O'Mara.

Paddock accepted his five cards and

looked at them. He raised his glance and let it rest on O'Mara's face.

O'Mara was a different man from the sullen, morosely brooding one of two nights before. And Paddock suddenly understood something that had not previously occurred to him. O'Mara, along with all the other troopers at Fort Phil Kearny, needed more than building, than work, to keep up their morale.

They needed action — the kind they'd had yesterday. In its absence they needed drill, long hours of it every day. These men weren't carpenters. They were soldiers and they needed to keep busy at their trade.

Paddock threw down three cards, called the bet and drew three more. He had drawn another eight, which gave him three.

O'Mara was studying him. Paddock tried to look disgusted. He threw down his hand.

The other players stayed. O'Mara won the pot.

The deal passed to Lance Corporal Kelly. He dealt the cards deftly. Paddock looked wryly at the ones he now held, and couldn't help grinning to himself. When a man wanted to lose, it seemed to be damned near impossible. He had two pair, queens and tens.

The dealer called for openers, and Paddock put a dollar into the pot. They'd know he had jacks or better, but they wouldn't know he had a second pair.

Two dropped out. The other two stayed, O'Mara one of them. Paddock checked the bet.

O'Mara bet five dollars and put a gold piece into the pot. Paddock folded; the other player called. Again O'Mara won the pot.

Paddock wasn't foolish enough to think that letting O'Mara win his money back would end the trouble between him and the sergeant. O'Mara was quarrelsome and unforgiving and his army record was one long chronicle of drunkenness, brawling and insubordination. He had made sergeant and been broken back half a dozen times. He was no stranger to the inside of the guardhouse. His nose had been broken and flattened and he was missing several of his teeth. His ears were twisted and misshapen as a result of repeated blows.

But Paddock also knew that he would be gone in less than a month. If he could placate O'Mara that long, he might not have to fight the man again.

CHAPTER 9

Paddock won despite his trying not to win. He knew he couldn't fold every time without arousing suspicion. He had to play a few of the hands dealt to him. And it seemed that every time he decided to play a hand, he held the winning one.

O'Mara's temper steadily grew worse. He glared at Paddock every time Paddock bet. At last, around ten o'clock, Paddock had enough. He raked his winnings into his hat and rose to go.

O'Mara growled, "Quittin' winners again, Bucko?"

Angrily Paddock slammed the hat back down on the table. He said, "All right. One hand. For everything in the hat."

"Count it."

Paddock dumped the hat out on the table and counted the money. There was a little over fifty-seven dollars. O'Mara counted what money he had left in front of him. He borrowed several dollars from the man on his right, more from the man beyond. Another sergeant, who was not in

95

the game, loaned him the rest. O'Mara counted it and pushed the money into the center of the table.

Paddock knew this was a hand he didn't dare win. He said, "Wait a minute, I said one hand. I didn't say showdown."

O'Mara shrugged and pulled his money back. One of the other men shuffled the cards and Paddock cut. The man dealt and Paddock picked up his cards. He had three aces, a five and a four. He looked questioningly at O'Mara.

O'Mara pushed a five-dollar gold piece into the center of the table. Paddock called it. He discarded two of the aces, keeping the third one, a four and a five. He drew two cards and looked at them. One was an ace.

He looked at O'Mara. "Bet 'em."

Even though they were playing only one hand, O'Mara hesitated a fraction of an instant. He had opened and had drawn three cards, so Paddock knew he had at least a pair of Jacks. He could have no more than a pair of kings. His hesitation now betrayed him. His draw had not bettered his hand.

He shoved another five into the pot. Paddock said, "We're playing one hand for the pile. Bet it all."

O'Mara nodded and shoved what money

was left in front of him into the pot. Paddock let his breath sigh slowly out. O'Mara couldn't have three of a kind. He wouldn't have hesitated about betting if he had. He could have a second pair, but Paddock didn't think so. He himself probably had the winning hand and he didn't dare turn it up.

He shoved his own money out into the pot and looked at O'Mara. "You're called. What've you got?"

O'Mara turned over a pair of kings. Paddock slammed his own hand face down on top of the deck. He said disgustedly, "I thought you had jacks. I had queens myself."

He hoped nobody would look at his cards. He reached disgustedly for the deck to shuffle, but O'Mara beat him to it. He flipped over the top five cards.

Paddock got to his feet, thinking, "Here it comes!"

O'Mara's face lost color, and then turned a dark and angry red. He scowled at Paddock. Quickly he flipped the cards back over and began to shuffle them.

Paddock glanced at the faces of the other men, wondering if they had seen the cards. He thought they had but they didn't say anything. Nor did O'Mara.

Paddock met the sergeant's glance steadily. He glanced down at the pot, wondering if O'Mara would refuse it or pick it up. O'Mara raked it over the edge of the table into his hat.

Paddock grunted, "Good-night," and shrugged into his coat.

One or two of the men answered him. O'Mara did not. He just glared at Paddock malevolently.

Paddock tramped disgustedly out into the night. He had tried to better things between O'Mara and himself and he'd only made them worse. O'Mara might have forgiven him for losing deliberately, if it had remained between the two of them. It hadn't. The others who had been in the game had to have seen the cards O'Mara turned over. They knew Paddock had lost deliberately and they knew why.

He went into his quarters, lighted the lamp and angrily slammed the door. He built up the fire and began to pace nervously back and forth.

He supposed that when a man is determined to quarrel, there is not much that can be done short of accommodating him. He would have to fight O'Mara. Sooner or later, out behind the stables, he'd have to fight the sergeant in a bruising marathon that couldn't end until one or both of them lay unconscious on the ground. Or until one was dead.

Finally, nervous and knowing he wouldn't sleep unless he did, he got a brown bottle out of a drawer and poured a glass half full. He gulped the whisky then took off his shirt, pants and boots. He blew out the lamp and got into bed. He placed his revolver within reach of his hand on the floor, even though he doubted if O'Mara would show up again. O'Mara had the money and unless he was bent on outright murder there'd be no point in his coming here.

He hadn't expected to sleep but he did. He didn't stir until reveille sounded out on the cold, wind-swept parade.

He had his breakfast in the teamster's mess as usual, then went out and walked toward the parade. He did not see Molly Benedict.

As he reached the corner of the stables, the bugler sounded Officers' Call. Immediately thereafter, Lt. Wands, who was apparently Officer of the Day, crossed the parade toward him. The sun was up this morning and was welcome even though it gave off little warmth. Wands said, "Colonel Carrington wants to see you in his quarters, Jess."

"What's up?"

"A rehash of what happened day before yesterday, I suppose. He's got to file a report."

Wands didn't say it, but Paddock knew what he was thinking. Carrington wanted to word his report in such a way that it would not later be challenged by his officers.

Collar up around his ears against the bitter wind, Paddock followed Wands across the parade to Carrington's small log house. Other officers were leaving their own quarters in response to the bugle call. Paddock followed Grummond in, and Fetterman came in immediately behind, closely followed by Capt. Brown.

Carrington nodded pleasantly enough to Paddock, but he seemed worried and preoccupied. It was clear he felt the hostility of his junior officers, whose greetings were correct and nothing more.

When everybody had arrived, the colonel said, "I am writing my report of the engagement day before yesterday. I want your thoughts on what happened and I want to know why you think we failed in what we tried to do." He looked at Fetterman, who seemed subdued. "Colonel?"

Fetterman shook his head. Captain Brown jumped to his feet. "Colonel, there were several reasons why we failed. I doubt if they're important now. What is important is that the Sioux whipped us and, except for luck, would have whipped us worse. We can't let that go unchallenged, Colonel. If we do, we're finished here."

Carrington asked drily, "And what would you suggest, Captain Brown?"

"They need to be taught a lesson, Colonel. They need to be taught that we can whip them any time we please."

"You're suggesting another expedition against the Indians?"

Brown's eyes glowed and he got to his feet. "Exactly. Let me take sixty of the civilians, Colonel. Sixty with revolvers and repeating rifles. And give me forty mounted troopers with repeating rifles. By the Lord, Colonel, we'll show those Sioux a thing or two. We'll ride to the Tongue River and burn their villages and scatter their pony herds. And I promise you, Colonel, they'll not bother this fort again."

Carrington glanced at the younger officers. "Lieutenant Wands?"

"I'll be proud to go along with Captain Brown, sir."

"Fetterman?"

Fetterman's lethargy seemed less. He said, "Glad to go, Colonel, if you authorize the expedition."

Paddock stared closely at Fetterman. He thought he knew why Fetterman seemed so subdued. Fetterman had, day before yesterday, stared defeat and death squarely in the face and the experience had shaken him. He had been so sure, Paddock thought, that he could ride through the whole Sioux nation with a hundred men. But that had been before he saw the thousands of howling Indians out there in the hills. Now he was not so sure.

His confidence would return, of course. He was a professional soldier. Carrington looked at Capt. Ten Eyck. "Captain?"

Ten Eyck asked wryly, "Are you going to authorize such an expedition, sir, or are you just sounding us out?"

Carrington showed him the faintest of smiles. "Sounding you out, Captain. I'm not going to authorize such an expedition. At least not now."

Brown's face had reddened. He said, "Colonel, you can't be serious! Those dirty-blanket Indians have beaten us. If we don't get out and avenge that defeat, they'll be coming over the stockade next."

Carrington asked, "Did you see how many of those 'dirty-blanket Indians' there were?"

"Am I to gather from that, Colonel, that you are afraid?"

It was Carrington's turn to flush. His eyes glowed with anger. Paddock had never seen him so furious. "Captain, are you accusing me of cowardice?"

Brown never got a chance to reply. Lt. Grummond broke in intemperately, "Colonel, why didn't you attack the Indians' rear day before yesterday according to the plan? And when you saw Lieutenant Bingham and me and the three men we took with us to protect your flank engaged, why didn't you come to our aid?"

Carrington's face lost some of its angry color. He was trying hard to maintain his control. He said, "Lieutenant, I didn't attack the Indians' rear because I never got an opportunity. The last I saw of Fetterman, he was chasing the Indians and I was afraid he was going so fast he'd get ahead of me and I'd never get the chance to attack the Indians' rear. I didn't know Fetterman got pinned down when Bingham and his cavalry ran away."

"Then why didn't you support Lieutenant Bingham and myself when we were attacked trying to protect your flank?"

"Because I knew nothing about it. I gave you no orders, Lieutenant Grummond, to attack Indians on my flank. I couldn't see you and I had no way of knowing you were under attack."

Carrington was still angry, and the accusation of cowardice obviously still rankled him. Paddock wondered how many commanding officers would tolerate this kind of abuse from their junior officers.

Perhaps it was Carrington's own uncertainty as to his qualifications that kept him from ruthlessly asserting his authority. He was not a combat officer. His war service had been behind a desk.

Grummond subsided into angry grumbling. Carrington looked challengingly around the room. "Anybody else got anything to say?"

Paddock said, "I'd like to put in my two cents worth. The way I see it, Bingham made the biggest mistake the other day. You can't retreat from Indians, Colonel. The minute you do they're all over you. When Bingham broke and ran, it gave the Sioux the encouragement they needed. I think we're lucky we came out of it as well as we did. The whole command could have been wiped out if the Indians had been organized better than they were."

Carrington nodded. "Thank you, Mr. Paddock."

None of the other officers commented on what Paddock had said. Most of them looked irritated because he'd had the temerity to speak at all.

Carrington said, "All right, gentlemen, the subject is closed. I will write my report and send it in. I want no more discussion of what happened day before yesterday."

He glanced challengingly around the room. Then he said, "There will be some changes made, so that something worse won't happen sometime in the future. First, all troops will be drilled daily. There will be both close order drill and mounted drill. I would like to authorize target practice for every man. That is impossible because we have too little ammunition here to use it up practicing. But I want a perpetual state of readiness maintained. Cavalry mounts will be saddled every morning and left saddled all day in case it is necessary for us to leave the fort and rescue the wood train again. Cinches will be kept loose and bits out so that the horses can eat and drink. Is that clear, gentlemen?"

The response was less than respectful and consisted mostly of surly grumbling. Carrington caught Paddock's eye and the slightest of grins touched the corners of his mouth. He said, "Then that's all, gentlemen. But before you go, let me stress one thing.

Disobedience of my orders will result in court-martial for the guilty, be they officers or enlisted men."

The resentful grumbling was even more audible than before as the officers filed out into the cold.

Paddock watched them go, hat in hand, waiting his turn to go out the door. Carrington stopped him before he could. "I've got a funny feeling, Jess."

"About what, Colonel?"

"About this fort. About what may happen if we're not careful. That's an insubordinate bunch if ever I saw one."

Jess said, "Nothing's going to happen, Colonel. Just don't let them talk you into anything."

He stepped out into the cold, cramming his hat down on his head. He had reassured the colonel but he didn't feel reassured himself. Carrington's junior officers *were* insubordinate. And in their rebellion might lie the seeds of disaster for everyone.

CHAPTER 10

The days dragged past. It did not storm, but neither did it thaw. The wind blew ferociously, drifting the snow that still lay unmelted on the parade. It whistled endlessly around the eaves of the buildings, chilling anyone who ventured out. Occasionally the sun broke through the clouds but it had no warmth and never got more than halfway up the sky.

On the parade, the troops drilled, the commands of their sergeants audible in every corner of the fort. Cavalry horses trotted and galloped. Their riders practiced repeatedly the command to dismount and fight on foot, and the shout, "Horse holders!" became a familiar one.

Jess saw Molly at least once a day, sometimes more. It became routine for him to carry her buckets to the water gate every morning and fill them for her. It became as routine for him to have coffee with her each night just before Taps sounded on the parade.

His uneasiness remained. The ingredients

of trouble all were present here at Kearny. Boredom. Isolation. The ever-present menace of the horde of hostile Indians outside the stockade. The insubordinate junior officers inside.

And in spite of all the drill, drinking and brawling among the men was as prevalent as before. Colored Susan did a thriving business in contraband whisky, particularly among the NCOs who had more money to spend on it than the privates did. The guardhouse held twice the number of occupants its design called for and more were being sentenced to it every day.

Sergeant O'Mara hardly seemed to draw a sober breath. Twice within a week he fought another NCO in back of the stables, both times beating the other unmercifully. Every time he saw Paddock he scowled and met Paddock's glance with malevolent promise. Paddock knew that sooner or later the sergeant would force him into a fight.

It finally happened on the morning of the 17th of December. Paddock was walking past the NCO quarters with Molly, carrying the last load of water, when O'Mara, unshaven and red-eyed, came out of his quarters and stood on the walk, not a dozen yards away. His voice was loud and its challenge was unmistakable. "Well now, how is it you're goin' to be paid for all that work, Bucko?"

Paddock glanced at O'Mara, then at Molly Benedict. Her face was very pale. She said. "It is all right, Jess. He is only baiting you."

"I know. But it's not all right." He put the buckets down and walked to O'Mara. Molly hurriedly picked them up and went on with them.

Paddock said, "I wondered when you'd get around to it. Do you want it here and now, or do you want it behind the stables later on?"

O'Mara grinned. "The stables, Bucko. I don't want to be interrupted when I go to work on you."

Paddock nodded. "This afternoon?"

"Two o'clock. The men'll be drillin' on the parade an' it'll not be so likely the officers will hear."

Paddock nodded. He turned and walked away. Molly had disappeared into her cabin but when he approached, she opened the door for him. Her face was worried. "Jess, you're not going to fight him?"

"No way out of it. If I was to back away, he'd make life miserable for both of us."

"He's vicious. He'll kill you if he can."

He knew her husband had been killed in just such a fight at Fort Laramie. He said, "I can handle him."

"Are you so sure you can? My husband thought he could handle the man he fought with too. But he couldn't handle a pitchfork driven into his chest. And it didn't help that the man who did it was sentenced to twenty years."

Paddock said, "Molly, I can't get out of it. There's no way. But I'll be careful."

She stared at him exasperatedly, hands on her shapely hips. "Why is pride so important to a man?"

Paddock grinned, shrugging slightly as he did. "Nature of the critter, I suppose. But without it, a man's not much."

"When is it to be?"

"This afternoon. At two o'clock."

"I could go to Colonel Carrington. I could have it stopped."

"But you won't."

"How do you know I won't?"

His smile faded. "Don't do it, Molly. Don't interfere."

"Should I let you get yourself killed rolling around in stable dirt? Is that what you want from me?" Tears were very close behind her eyes and her chin was trembling.

Paddock crossed the room and took her

in his arms. She began to cry, softly, almost silently. He said, "Molly, it will be all right."

She pulled angrily away. "Damn you. Oh damn you, Jess Paddock, for being such a stubborn mule!" She turned her back to him and busied herself at the stove. He could see her shoulders shaking.

He wanted to comfort her but knew that he could not. He opened the door and stepped out into the wind, closing it quickly behind him.

He hesitated a moment on the stoop, then strode rapidly away. He could feel a kind of emptiness in his stomach. It was always this way just before a fight, whether the fight be one with fists or a more serious duel with guns. Today it seemed even worse, perhaps because he knew the unpredictability of the man he was to fight. O'Mara was not above using a pitchfork if he could lay his hands on one. Or an ax. Or a singletree.

But the waiting would be the worst part of it. It now was only half past eight and the fight was to be at two. Six hours of waiting. Six hours, while tension grew each minute until by the time the fight began it would be almost intolerable.

For a while, he paced nervously back

and forth inside his room. Unable to stand the confinement any more, he went out, walked along the frozen street until he came to the parade. He stood watching the troopers drill until the wind had chilled him to the bone. He looked at his watch. It was still not ten o'clock.

He went into the sutler's store and drank a beer. He idly watched a poker game between four civilians for a while. He went back and had another beer. Returning, he got into the game and it diverted him until noon, though he neither won nor lost.

He walked to the teamsters' mess. Everybody seemed to know about the fight and Paddock wondered curiously how the news had managed to get around so fast. He had told no one and Molly certainly hadn't. O'Mara must have spread the word. He grinned at a teamster named Larabee and asked, "What are the odds by now?"

The man grinned back. "Five to three on O'Mara, Jess."

Paddock pulled out three ten-dollar gold pieces. "Get me some of that. And take my advice. Bet some yourself."

"You think you can take him, Jess? He's tough and he's mean as hell."

"I can take him, Larabee. Go lay that bet."

Larabee left. Paddock knew he would bet the thirty dollars against O'Mara but he couldn't be sure Larabee would place any of his own money the same way.

He ate sparingly. Afterward he took a rapid turn around the perimeter of the fort. When he finished he was breathing faster and he was sweating a little underneath his coat. The fight would start fast and he wanted to be warmed up when it did.

It was half past one when he reached the appointed place. It was a large area, bounded on the northwest by the cavalry stables, on the southwest by a row of incomplete NCO quarters, used in the interim as cavalry barracks and on the remaining two sides by a secondary stockade. In all, the area was a hundred and fifty by three hundred feet, but not all of that was open space. Wagons, buckboards, buggies and ambulances were drawn up against the stockade on the southeast side. A tackroom and saddler's workshop took up a corner near the partially constructed NCO quarters.

Forty or fifty men, both troopers and civilians, were waiting for the fight to start. Paddock saw several bets change hands. One man seemed to be booking bets from all comers. He held a thick wad of paper money in one hand, a bag of gold in the other. Beside him stood a man with pencil and paper, recording the bets he made.

All the men present studied Paddock speculatively, and he grinned faintly to himself. O'Mara was already here, stripped to the waist, the upper half of his red-flannel underwear drooping below his waist, the sleeves tied behind his back. O'Mara's chest was like a barrel and was covered with a thick mat of rust-colored hair. Even his back had hair on it.

He was dancing around in a circle, feinting with his fists at an imaginary foe. Paddock handed his hat to a trooper standing nearby and followed it with his coat. He did not strip as O'Mara had. He said, "Let's get on with it."

O'Mara bared his teeth. He said, "Anything goes, Bucko."

Paddock shrugged. He had no idea how he was going to fight this man. He'd have to wait and see what O'Mara's style of fighting was.

O'Mara didn't make him wait very long. Lowering his head, he came charging across the cleared area. His arms were outstretched, grappling for Paddock, who stepped aside at the last moment and brought both hands, clasped together to make a single outsized fist, down on the back of O'Mara's neck with all the force he could command. O'Mara made no sound. He pitched forward, his face skidding on the manure-covered, frozen ground. He groaned, and rolled, and fought to his hands and knees, looking over his shoulder and up at Paddock who was approaching to administer a kick while he still was down.

Before Paddock reached him, he pushed himself to hands and knees and then to his feet. The arrogance was gone now from his face, replaced by wariness. He stood, swaying slightly, playing for time to let the effects of Paddock's blow wear off.

Paddock bored in, slamming a fist into O'Mara's gut. O'Mara doubled with the force of it, but as he staggered forward, he caught Paddock around the waist with both arms before Paddock could retreat. Bending his thick body forward, he tightened the grip of his short and powerful arms until Paddock, bent backward like a bow, felt ribs and spine crack, and cried out involuntarily with the pain of it.

He tried to twist, but O'Mara's grip was too powerful. The breath of the man was strong and hot against his face, reeking of the rot-gut whisky Colored Susan sold. O'Mara was chuckling triumphantly, as if the fight was already won.

Paddock let himself fall backward by kicking his feet free of the ground. Both men crashed down. Falling, Paddock brought a knee slamming up into O'Mara's groin and felt the sergeant's grip loosen slightly. The knee expelled a grunt of pain from him. Paddock twisted violently. He did not succeed in breaking O'Mara's terrible grip, but he turned inside it, so that his back was to the sergeant. Grabbing both O'Mara's hands now with his own, he flung himself to one side at the same time dragging O'Mara's clasped hands across the rough and hard-frozen ground.

Skin peeled from O'Mara's knuckles, leaving them bleeding and raw. He released Paddock, and Paddock rolled clear, coming to his feet as O'Mara swung a long, looping right that caught him squarely on the side of the head.

Stunned, he retreated, covering with elbows and forearms. O'Mara bored in recklessly. When O'Mara was open, Paddock stopped, set himself, and buried a fist in O'Mara's bulging belly, driving another painful grunt of breath from him.

He was angered now, angered enough to

stand flatfooted and trade punches with the sergeant. Slugging savagely, taking as much as he gave, he soon had a torn ear, a flattened nose, a swelling eye and a badly bruised and bleeding mouth.

Both men breathed rapidly, blowing out a huge cloud of steam with each breath exhaled. Paddock's head was ringing from O'Mara's blows but the sergeant seemed unaffected by the ones he had landed and Paddock knew O'Mara was going to outlast him if he continued to fight this way. He stepped back, ducking and weaving and relying on footwork to keep him from getting hit.

O'Mara growled, "Fight, ye sonofabitch."

Paddock didn't waste breath on a reply. He heard someone in the crowd yell, "Two to one on O'Mara, lads!" and thought ruefully that he must be getting the worst of it or the odds wouldn't have changed that much. O'Mara rushed at him and now he waited until the man was less than half a dozen feet away before he plunged ahead. His fist caught O'Mara squarely on the nose and it burst like a tomato, showering blood on both Paddock and O'Mara as it did.

Stopped and bloodied, eyes streaming, hurt at last, O'Mara let out a bellow and charged. Paddock stepped aside, once more slamming down both clasped hands on the back of O'Mara's neck as he went past. Once more, O'Mara skidded face down in the frozen manure, only stopping after he had plunged into and scattered a part of the crowd.

His head slammed into a broken singletree, half-buried in the frozen ground. Stunned, he fought to his hands and knees. Seizing the half-buried singletree, he wrenched it loose and rose with it grasped solidly in both his hands. Frozen clods still clung to it. O'Mara growled. "Now, ye sonofabitch, I'll bust yer head like a rotten punkin."

Paddock waited, balanced lightly on the balls of his feet. A quick glance around had revealed nothing that might even the odds. O'Mara came on, and, half a dozen feet away, set himself to swing the singletree.

Paddock saw it start and knew if it struck him, it would break bones wherever it happened to land. Ready for it, he ducked as it started, too late for O'Mara to change the direction of its swing.

It whistled overhead, less than an inch away, and Paddock straightened immediately. The momentum of the club swung O'Mara halfway around. Paddock closed with him and seized the singletree as it completed its circle. He wrenched it out of O'Mara's hands and poised to strike.

Something stopped him. It wasn't gallantry and it wasn't a conviction that the singletree was unfair. It was, instead, both the knowledge that he could kill O'Mara with the thing and the further knowledge that beating O'Mara this way wouldn't solve anything. Stepping back, he flung it into the air, over the heads of the crowd and beyond, where O'Mara couldn't get his hands on it again. He turned and faced O'Mara, prepared now to do this the hard way, prepared to stand toe to toe and slug it out with the other man.

O'Mara came boring in, surprised, but as willing as Paddock was.

Time lost meaning and became a blur of weariness and pain. Paddock slugged until he couldn't raise his hands, until each breath was a red hot flame searing his lungs and throat. He sank to his knees, dimly aware that O'Mara was also on his knees but still he swung his fists, though each blow now took half a minute to start and land.

His head whirled and he felt himself falling and he thought dimly that he had lost the fight. But no more blows landed and somewhere he could hear someone groaning and after a while a bucket of icy water was thrown directly into his face.

Gasping and choking but partially revived, he struggled to his hands and knees. O'Mara lay on his back, gasping like a fish out of water. Men helped him to his feet and others helped Paddock up and he heard someone shout, "All bets are off! It ended in a draw!"

With a man supporting him on each side, he let himself be led away toward his quarters. Someone gave him a bottle and he drank, his smashed lips burning like fire as he did. He fell back on his bed and suddenly he knew no more.

CHAPTER 11

When Paddock awoke, it was to look into Molly Benedict's eyes. She was sitting beside his bed, gently bathing the lacerations on his face with a warm, wet cloth. Seeing he was awake, she said spiritedly, "Well, I am glad to see you are alive."

A lamp was burning and he realized he had been unconscious all afternoon. Molly's voice had betrayed impatience, but her glance, resting on his face, was soft. He asked, "What time is it?"

"Ten o'clock."

"And I've been asleep all that time?"

"You have."

For an instant there was silence. At last she asked, "What did it prove? If the stories I have heard are true, neither of you won. So what was the use of it?"

He grinned. "I guess women find something like that hard to understand." His grin widened and his scabbed, split lips hurt as a result. "But then there are one or two things about women that men find equally hard to understand."

A reluctant smile touched her mouth. "All right. Anyway, it's over. Do you want something to eat?"

He nodded.

"I have some soup simmering on the stove over at my place. Do you want to come over, or do you want me to bring it here?"

He said, "Give me ten minutes to change my clothes."

She got to her feet, hesitated a moment, then put on her coat and went out the door. Paddock struggled to his feet, feeling the ache in every muscle, in every bone. Wincing with each movement, he took off his shirt, boots and pants. He found clean clothes and put them on. Shrugging painfully into his coat and cramming on his hat, he went out into the everlasting wind.

Head down, he hurried to Molly's door. She opened it at his knock and he went inside.

The soup smelled delicious and he realized he was ravenous. Eating was difficult because of his smashed mouth, but he put away two bowls of soup and several pieces of bread. Finished, he thanked her and went back to his own room. This time he stripped to his underwear before getting into bed. He was almost instantly asleep and did not even stir at reveille. A loud knocking on his door roused him about an hour afterward.

It was Col. Carrington's servant, Black George. Paddock stood shivering in the icy wind blowing through the open doorway and asked, "What is it, George?"

"Colonel Carrington say he want to see you, suh. Soon's you kin make it. It's impo'tant, the colonel says."

"All right. I'll be there in twenty minutes or so."

"Yessuh." George hurried away and Paddock closed the door.

Moving still hurt him but not as much as it had the night before. Quickly he washed and shaved and tugged on his coat. Putting on his hat, he hurried out.

Molly was carrying her own water this morning. She was just entering her house with the last two buckets. He waved to her but he didn't stop to talk.

Carrington was waiting. Paddock closed the door behind him and crossed the room to put his back to the glowing stove. Carrington looked at his bruised and lacerated face for several moments before he asked, "How do you feel?"

"I'll live."

Carrington nodded, by his nod dismissing

the subject. "I'd like you to make a scout." He grinned faintly. "There is always the chance I'll be pressured into going out again."

"When do you want me to go?"

"Today. Tonight. Whenever you think it's fairly safe."

Paddock said, "It'd be suicide to go out of here in daylight. They've got pickets watching every move we make. But I could go out tonight and stay out all day tomorrow and come in again tomorrow night."

"All right."

"What do you want to know?"

"How many Indians there are now in the vicinity of the fort. What they're doing and what they're planning, if you can tell. If they're going to attack the fort, I'd like to know ahead of time. If they're just waiting for us to come out, I want to know that too."

Paddock nodded. Carrington said, "I need that information, Paddock, so don't do anything foolish."

Paddock shook his head. "I won't."

"How will you keep from getting caught?"

"Why, I'll wear moccasins and go out afoot. I'll find me a high point before dawn and hole up there for the day. I won't move until it gets dark again."

"All right, Jess. Good luck."

Paddock went out the door. He intended to sleep all day if he could. He'd be awake all night tonight and all day tomorrow. Head down, he hurried toward his quarters, deciding on the way that he wouldn't tell Molly what he was going to do. There was no use worrying her and he couldn't change what he had to do.

He waited that night until after ten o'clock. He kissed Molly lightly at her door and heard it close behind him. He hurried to his own quarters then and put on the moccasins he kept for just such an eventuality as this.

At the sutler's store he got a sack of grub. He got a plug of chewing tobacco but left his pipe behind, knowing its smell could get him killed.

Armed with rifle and revolver and plenty of ammunition for both, he left the fort by climbing the banquette and vaulting over the top of the stockade. He didn't want to risk the squeak the gates made opening.

Outside the stockade, he crouched a moment, listening. All he could hear was the endless whistling of the wind. Slowly and soundlessly, he edged along the stockade until came to the bed of Little

Piney Creek. Following this and staying hidden in the brush, he worked his way down to the point where the two creek branches joined.

He hated getting wet but he knew there was no help for it. He crouched silently in the brush for a while, listening. Deciding it was safe, he removed his moccasins and pants. Carrying them he waded out into the icy water, breaking the crust of ice ahead of him with one hand. He was shivering violently from the cold when he reached the other side and his teeth were chattering.

He squeezed as much of the water out of his lower underwear as he could, then put on his pants and moccasins. After that he moved out briskly along the rutted Bozeman Road.

He trotted for about a mile before his feet and legs felt warm again. Drawing off to the side of the road and down the slope into a clump of pines, he waited silently, watching the road in the direction of the fort.

He did not have to wait long. Two Indians came trotting up the road. They stopped not a dozen yards away and conversed briefly in the Dakota tongue. After that they went on, but more slowly and cautiously than before.

They had seen him, or heard him, he thought, trotting up the Bozeman Road trying to take the chill out of his legs and feet. But they weren't sure who he was or even that he wasn't another Indian and they'd give up the pursuit when they failed to find any trace of him.

He stayed where he was, crouched and silent, for almost an hour before he dared to move again. His legs were still damp, and they had chilled and turned stiff with the inactivity. He hoped they'd be thoroughly dry before daylight came because after that he wouldn't dare to move around at all.

Finally, deciding the two Indians had gone back to their camp, he climbed cautiously up to the road. He did not stay on it, however, deciding it was less safe than the hillside since the Indians were prone to use it going back and forth. Instead, he moved down onto the northern slope of Lodge Trail Ridge.

There were times when traveling silently was impossible. Crossing patches of crusted snow, his feet made what seemed like thunderous crunching sounds breaking through. In complete darkness, his feet snapped twigs and occasionally dislodged rocks.

He stopped every hundred yards or so to

listen intently and sometimes he halted unexpectedly, trying to catch the sounds of someone following. He heard nothing but the endless sighing of the wind in the pines and the muted roar of Big Piney Creek far below.

There was little danger in traveling this slope of Lodge Trail Ridge, he thought. No pickets would be stationed here because from here the fort wasn't visible. Indians not on picket duty would be in camp, probably sleeping because the hour was very late.

At last, nearly four hours after leaving the fort, he reached a high point on Lodge Trail Ridge that he remembered from the other day. From it he knew the fort was visible. He could also see into the valley of Big Piney Creek, and beyond the northern tip of the Sullivant Hills, into the drainage of Little Piney Creek, where the wood road was.

Looking the other way, north, he would be able to see a long stretch of the valley of Peno Creek.

There was a jumble of rocks here at the crest of Lodge Trail Ridge, but instead of concealing himself in them he chose to climb a thick pine, knowing that the Indians were likely to make use, at some time tomorrow, of this high vantage point. Indians were no more likely to look up into nearby trees than white men were and he judged it to be the safest place.

He climbed about two-thirds of the way to the top, and here found a branch about three inches thick upon which he could comfortably sit. A lower branch made an excellent place for him to put his feet. He felt exposed and vulnerable and he knew that if one of the Indians happened to spot him, there would be no chance to escape. They'd shoot him out of the tree the way a hunter shoots a lion his dogs have treed.

Leaning against the trunk, his rifle across his knees, he closed his eyes and tried to sleep.

But sleep eluded him. His body still ached from the pounding O'Mara had given him the day before yesterday. His underwear was still damp from wading across the creek and the wind, up here in the trees, was cold and had an unbroken sweep for miles.

Dawn came finally, gray and cheerless and even colder than the night had been. Faintly he heard the clear notes of the bugle at the fort calling reveille.

It was a long time before he saw anything. Then it was a deer, picking its way daintily up the slope toward him. The deer passed beneath his tree and went on.

A bluejay lit on a branch below him, saw him and flew away again with a raucous squawk. Paddock pulled out his watch. It was nine o'clock. He glanced toward the fort and saw the gates swing open. The wood train came rolling out, its wagons looking like toys at this distance. He counted them. There were fourteen. They headed northwest along the wood road and shortly disappeared behind the Sullivant Hills.

Now he swept the horizons carefully with his glance. A file of Indians came up the valley of the west fork of Peno Creek. There were, he guessed, several hundred of them. More came riding over the ridge from the east fork of Peno Creek. They grouped on the relatively flat valley floor, some galloping back and forth, yelling and making imaginary passes at an imaginary enemy. They seemed to be waiting for something and at last Paddock saw what it was. A chief, accompanied by several others, probably lesser chiefs or medicine men, came up the valley and as soon as he reached them, they clustered around to listen to what he had to say.

He harangued them for a long time,

gesturing as he talked. Paddock could neither hear his voice nor tell what the gestures meant, but shortly a group of fifty or sixty detached themselves from the others and galloped away over the divide separating the Peno Creek drainage from that of Big Piney Creek. He glimpsed them again going over the Sullivant Hills and he understood that they were heading for the Pinery to attack the wood train that had left the fort earlier.

Now the ominous meaning of the Indian gathering became plain to him. The Indians had done something Indians rarely do. They had formulated a battle plan. They had laid a trap and baited it with the fifty or sixty who had gone to attack the wood train from the fort.

There was nothing Paddock could do but watch. More Indians kept trickling over the ridge and up out of the valley of Peno Creek, until Paddock judged there must be well over a thousand down there in all. Suddenly they split, about half of them retiring back down into the valley of Peno Creek, the other half moving in a body east, over the saddle separating the two forks of Peno Creek and beyond, past the Bozeman Road and into the heavily wooded hills beyond.

Paddock stared, fascinated. All the Indians had now disappeared and he strained his ears, waiting for the sound of gunfire from the direction of the Pinery. For an instant he debated trying to get back to the fort, but he knew it would be no use. By the time he reached it, this drama would have played itself out to its inevitable, tragic end.

CHAPTER 12

Paddock scanned the landscape in all directions. Not an Indian was in sight. The wind still blew briskly toward him out of the northwest, from the direction of the Pinery. Although the distance was almost three miles, the sound of gunfire carried clearly, if faintly to his ears. The Sioux had attacked the wood detail.

He fixed his eyes on the fort. He was too far away to clearly see what was going on inside the log stockade, but once he thought he caught the faint notes of a bugle call and, fifteen minutes after hearing the first gunfire, he saw the gates swing wide.

A column of cavalry rode out at a swift canter and headed along the wood road toward the Pinery. In minutes they had disappeared behind the Sullivant Hills.

Paddock realized he was shivering, and it was not entirely from the cold. He would soon know if the commander of the relief column was going to take the Indians' bait.

He did not have long to wait. The fifty or

sixty Indians who had been dispatched to attack the wood train suddenly appeared on the crest of the Sullivant Hills, riding at a gallop as though pursued.

Paddock muttered to himself, "No! Don't do it! Don't follow them!" He was sure Col. Carrington would have given the commander of the relief column specific orders not to pursue the Indians over the Sullivant Hills and if the commander did pursue, it would be in direct disobedience of those orders. But Paddock also knew Brown's and Fetterman's eagerness, and he knew that both believed in the adage that disobedience of orders was never punished if distinction was achieved.

He realized suddenly that he was holding his breath. He let it exhale but he did not take his eyes off the crest of the Sullivant Hills where the relief column would appear if its commander had decided to pursue the Indians.

Several minutes passed. Paddock slowly relaxed. By now, the fleeing Indians had reached the valley of Big Piney Creek and were splashing across the stream. They had slowed their horses to a walk. On the east side of Big Piney Creek, they stopped and their horses milled uncertainly as their riders stared back in the direction they had come.

Paddock grinned with his relief. He watched the Sioux braves ride up the side of Lodge Trail Ridge and thence down into the valley of the west fork of Peno Creek, following the route taken by Fetterman's cavalry on December 6th. They climbed the saddle separating the two forks and halted there again.

Now the two concealed forces of Indians came suddenly into sight. Like a swarm of ants they came riding from right and left to join the decoy force on the little ridge. They milled around for fifteen or twenty minutes, listening to their chiefs, before they rode slowly away down into the valley of Peno Creek and disappeared.

The trap had failed. Whoever had been in command of the force sent out to relieve the wood detail had obeyed his orders and done no more than drive the Indians off. Paddock looked back toward the fort and saw the wagons of the wood detail, accompanied by the troop of cavalry, come into sight from behind the Sullivant Hills. They reached the fort and entered it and the gates swung shut behind them.

Paddock dragged his watch from his pocket. It was only eleven o'clock. The whole operation had taken less than two hours. He'd have to remain here until dark but he already had the information Col. Carrington had sent him out to get. The Sioux had no intention of facing the artillery in a direct attack upon the fort. Their strategy was to lure a column of cavalry into their trap. The white soldiers might have learned something from their encounter with the Sioux December 6th, but the Sioux had also learned.

He got some dry biscuits and cooked meat from his grub sack and ate, afterward drinking water from his canteen. No sooner had he finished than he heard the sounds of horses approaching.

He froze and a few moments later saw two Indians come riding to the top of the ridge from the north. They were conversing in their own language. They dismounted, tied their horses and took up a position in the rocks below Paddock's tree.

He cursed sourly to himself. He doubted if they'd look up and discover him but their presence would mean he didn't dare to sleep. It would also mean he'd have to spend the rest of the day virtually motionless so that he wouldn't give himself away.

The Indians were watching the fort, but occasionally they would glance toward the Sullivant Hills as though expecting soldiers to appear suddenly at their crest.

The minutes and the hours dragged. Briefly the sun came out and then it went behind the clouds again. In mid-afternoon, the wind picked up, swaying the pine in which Paddock sat.

It was almost dusk when the Indians finally mounted their horses and rode away. Paddock remained where he was until full dark. Then, stiffly and carefully, he climbed down from his lofty perch.

He was chilled to the bone. He staggered and nearly fell when he tried to walk. Grumbling inwardly, he headed for the fort. It had been a long, hard night, and a longer, harder day. But he had the information he had been sent out to get.

He traveled with extreme care, knowing well the temptation to hurry when heading back. He stayed clear of the Bozeman Road, and once heard horses traveling on it. When he reached Big Piney Creek, he waded across at the same place he had crossed last night without bothering, this time, to remove his moccasins and pants.

Reaching the fort, he called to the sentry nearest the gate, "Open up, trooper. It's Paddock and I'm cold."

The gate swung open enough to permit his passage. He went in and headed for his quarters immediately. He lighted the lamp and, shivering, got out of his wet clothes and put dry ones on. The room was icy, having had no fire in it since yesterday. He built one and lighted it, then got a bottle of whisky and took a drink. Standing as close to the stove as he could, he took another, and another still.

The room was slow to warm, and Paddock stayed beside the stove until his pants began to scorch. Then he turned and scorched the other side. After that he took another drink, then left and headed for Colonel Carrington's house to make his report. He hoped Carrington would be alone, for he was in no mood to be scoffed at by Fetterman and Brown — and he was sure they would scoff at the conclusions he had reached.

Carrington was alone, except for his wife and Black George, both of whom left the room as soon as Paddock was admitted. Carrington looked at him and asked, "What did you find out?"

"Well, first of all, I don't think they're going to attack the fort."

"How do you know that?"

Paddock grinned. "Colonel, I watched them bait and set a trap. There were over a thousand of them. They sent fifty or so to attack the wood train and the rest of them split into two forces. One went down into the valley of Peno Creek and the other crossed the Bozeman Road. They stayed out of sight until the decoy force reached the saddle between the two forks of Peno Creek. If your relief force had followed the decoys, they'd have been cut off and slaughtered to a man. By the way, who did you send out to relieve the wood train?"

"Captain Powell. And I gave him explicit orders not to pursue the Indians over Lodge Trail Ridge."

Paddock grinned. "Good thing it wasn't Fetterman."

"Fetterman has never disobeyed his orders, Jess."

"That don't mean he won't. Well, anyway, I haven't closed my eyes for a day and a night and I'm damn near froze. I'm going to bed."

He stopped by Molly Benedict's house on the way to his own and told her where he had been. She looked at him exasperatedly but she didn't say anything about his having left without telling her. He hurried back to his own quarters and crawled into bed immediately. He did not awake until he heard reveille.

On that day, December 20th, Col.

Carrington decided to do something he had been considering for a long, long time. Every time the wood detail went out, it had to cross Big Piney Creek to get to the Pinery. Crossing, it was always extremely vulnerable to attack by the Indians. Today Carrington was going to build a bridge.

He left the fort about ten o'clock with a dozen wagons and forty or fifty men, half of whom were soldiers to protect the workmen while they cut the timber and built the bridge. Paddock went along, more out of curiosity than anything: would the detail be attacked this time?

At the crossing, Carrington sent a guarded wood-cutting detail into the woods while he remained at the bridge site to supervise the building of rock supports for the stringers in the center of the stream. Paddock sat his horse and smoked his pipe and waited for the Sioux.

Oddly, they did not appear. Once, he saw three pickets on the top of Lodge Trail Ridge, but they soon disappeared.

Carrington was a natural engineer, he thought, as he watched the work progress, and it was obvious that the colonel liked this kind of work. First he had a rock piling built in the middle of the stream. It was eighteen feet long and about six feet wide.

The rocks were contained by logs set upright like a stockade in the stream-bed. Because they could not be sunk very deeply into the rocky stream-bed they were held tight by chains passing all the way around them. Filled with rock, the enclosure made a solid base for the stringers that would support the bridge. These were logs slightly more than twenty-five feet long and a foot and a half thick at their base. They were skidded out into the stream with teams. The big ends, on both banks, were laid into trenches. The smaller ends were then lifted up onto the rock piling. In all, there were six supporting stringers, which should, Paddock thought, make a solid bridge.

Now workmen started from both banks and hewed the topsides of the stringers flat. As soon as this was completed, the three-inch sawed bridge planks were laid and nailed down with ten-inch spikes.

Paddock kept looking around for a sign of Indians, but he saw none. When the bridge was almost finished, and the sun low in the western sky, Carrington walked to where he sat. "Where are the Indians?"

Paddock shrugged. "Damned if I know where they are. Maybe they didn't figure we'd be out again today and they made no plans for it."

"Those three saw us here. They had time to go back for the others."

"I've been thinking that's what they did. But I guess I was wrong. They'd have been here by now."

"You couldn't have been mistaken about that trap?"

Paddock shook his head. "Not a chance, Colonel. Not a chance."

It was nearly dusk when the bridge was finished. The wagons rolled back toward the fort, with Paddock and Carrington riding behind. The bridge would take an hour off the wood train's time each day, half an hour going, half an hour coming back. Carrington was content and pleased with what had been accomplished.

But Paddock continued to watch the skyline, looking for the Sioux. He couldn't believe they had passed up this chance today after being disappointed yesterday. He wondered if disappointment and failure had started them to quarreling among themselves. He certainly hoped so — but he doubted it.

CHAPTER 13

It was now December 20th, and Paddock knew the supply train might arrive at any time. It would remain at the fort a day or two and would then return to Fort Laramie, under heavy escort. Among the soldiers and civilians who were also leaving, would go Paddock and Molly Benedict, as would Captain Brown, who was being transferred to Fort Laramie.

But for some reason, the imminence of the supply train's arrival failed to erase the worried look in Molly's eyes. Nor did Paddock's uneasiness disappear.

He left her house early that evening because he could see that she was tired, and he was thinking he would be glad when she could leave the heavy work she was doing here. He made his way thoughtfully to the sutler's store for pipe tobacco and a drink.

As he reached it, the door to Col. Carrington's house across the parade opened and he saw an officer step outside and come hurrying across the dark parade.

Paddock packed his pipe with the last of the tobacco in his pouch and lighted it, cupping the flame of the match against the wind. When the officer reached him he saw that it was Captain Brown. "Evening, Jess."

"Good-evening, Captain. It looks like another windy night."

"The damn wind never stops blowing here. If it was up to me, I'd say give it all back to the Indians."

Paddock said, "I'll buy you a drink."

"Thank you." Brown preceded him into the sutler's store and crossed to the bar. In the light, Paddock could see that he carried his customary two pistols and wore his spurs. Brown caught the direction of Paddock's glance and smiled a little self-consciously. "I'm going back to Laramie in a day or two and I want to be ready if the chance comes to go out and get myself an Indian scalp."

Paddock ordered a bottle and glasses and pushed the bottle toward Brown. Brown poured himself half a glass and passed the bottle back. He said, "It doesn't look like we're going to get another chance at the Indians before we leave, does it?"

Paddock grinned. "That will suit me. That will suit me fine."

Brown frowned, then with an effort forced a smile instead. "We will have to fight them eventually. There is not room here for both the Indians and the whites."

It was apparent to Paddock that Brown was trying to be agreeable. He poured himself a drink and raised his glass. "Your health, Captain."

Brown clinked his glass against Paddock's and both men drank. Brown said, "I take it you do not approve of our presence here."

Paddock said easily, "It's not my business to approve or disapprove, Captain. What's happening is inevitable. Sooner or later we'll have it all, no matter how we get it or what we have to do."

Brown frowned again, then changed the subject suddenly, saying, "My congratulations on your coming marriage to Mrs. Benedict."

"Thank you."

"What will you do? No more scouting I would suppose."

Paddock smiled and shook his head. "A ranch, I guess. I could never live in town."

Brown finished his drink. "Thank you, Jess. Good-night." He turned and left the sutler's store.

Paddock looked at Kinney. "Some pipe tobacco, John. Ridgewood."

Kinney got him a package. Paddock dumped the tobacco into his pouch and put the empty wrapping on the bar. He didn't want to leave. He realized that he didn't want to be alone and wondered why.

He paid for his tobacco and the drinks, told Kinney good night and left. Molly's house was dark.

He built up the fire in his own quarters and went to bed. His last thoughts were to wonder when the supply train would arrive, and why he had so dreaded, tonight, to leave the sutler's store and be alone.

The next day, December 21st, dawned clear and cold. While it still blew, the wind was not as strong as usual. The fort awakened to its daily business. Paddock carried Molly's water for her from the creek. After that, he climbed up on the banquette and stared southward along the Bozeman Road, wondering how far away the supply train was.

At ten, Carrington ordered the wood train out but, perhaps mindful of what Paddock had seen on scout, ordered a strong escort to accompany it, under the command of Corporal LeGrow. Counting soldiers and civilians, there were about ninety men.

The wagons creaked out the gate and headed for the Pinery. Paddock watched until they disappeared behind the knoll.

At eleven the picket on Pilot Hill signalled that the wagons were under attack by a large party of Indians and immediately the bugle sounded and troops began to assemble on the parade.

Frowning, Paddock watched, thinking of what he had seen from the tree on top of Lodge Trail Ridge. He saw a couple of Indian pickets ride into sight on Lodge Trail Ridge, dismount and sit down to watch the fort.

On the north side of Big Piney Creek four more Indians suddenly appeared and these began to shout epithets and obscenities at the soldiers inside the fort. Carrington, obviously annoyed, ordered three shots fired at them from a twelve-pound howitzer. The piece roared, flushing out about twenty more Indians from the road crossing when the shot exploded nearby. These and the other four fled northward, taking up positions near the first two on the slope of Lodge Trail Ridge, well out of range of the howitzers.

Col. Carrington roared, "Captain Powell!"

Powell mounted the horse that an orderly had just brought to him and rode to where

Carrington stood on the banquette. He saluted perfunctorily. Carrington said, "You will take fifty men, Captain, and relieve the wood train."

Powell again gave his perfunctory salute and rode away. Fetterman, also mounted, rode now to Carrington.

He saluted more briskly than the other, and Paddock heard him say, "Colonel Carrington, I claim seniority over Captain Powell. Let me take out the relief force, sir. I would think it was my right, particularly since Powell went out with it the other day."

Carrington stared at him doubtfully. Paddock could tell that the colonel was reluctant and knew exactly why. Carrington doubted Fetterman's reliability. He was afraid Fetterman, in his eagerness to whip the Indians, would disobey orders and ride away on his own.

At last Carrington nodded reluctantly. Fetterman grinned, saluted smartly and said, "Thank you, sir."

Carrington said, "Select your own command."

Fetterman rode out onto the parade, past the men assembled there. Paddock thought, "Oh hell," and ran for the stable to get his horse. Until now, he'd thought this was going to be routine and with Powell in command it would have been routine. But with Fetterman . . .

He glimpsed Molly standing on her stoop, shading her eyes with an upraised hand. He ran into the stables and quickly saddled up his horse. He rode back out to the parade.

Fetterman was in the process of selecting his command. Sitting his horse in front of his own Company A, he picked out twenty-one men by name. Moving on, he called out the names of nine more men from Company C, six of Company E and thirteen of Company H. All four companies belonged to the 18th Infantry. The men selected fell out, and reformed farther out on the parade in front of Colonel Fetterman's quarters, a force of fifty, counting Fetterman himself.

The guard was just being mounted and turned over to Lt. Wands, who was officer of the day.

Carrington beckoned to Fetterman and Fetterman rode once more to where he stood. There was an eagerness, or perhaps an impatience about him that was noticeable.

Curious, Paddock rode his horse closer to Carrington. Carrington was talking to Fetterman and Paddock caught the last of what he said. "Support the wood train. Relieve it and report to me. Do not engage or pursue Indians at its expense. Under no circumstances pursue over the ridge, as per map in your possession." The wording of Carrington's orders was excessively formal and Paddock understood that was so because Carrington suspected Fetterman might be tempted to disobey.

Fetterman's horse, as though his rider's excitement was contagious, was prancing, pulling at the bit, trying to rear. Fetterman rode back to his troops and sat for a moment looking them over, every inch the commander of cavalry, thought Paddock wryly to himself. Then, turning his horse and raising an arm, he waved the column forward and his shout, "Fo'ward, ho!" reached every corner of the fort.

Paddock glanced at Colonel Carrington. The post commander was frowning, and it was plain he understood Fetterman's thoughts just as well as Paddock had. Fetterman was going out for glory, going out to prove once and for all that he and Brown were right, Carrington wrong.

Paddock called, "Want me to go with him, Colonel?"

Carrington shook his head. "I may need you later, Jess," he said, and this was a betrayal of his anxiety that Fetterman would disregard the orders just given him. To Fetterman, as he rode past at the head of his troops, Carrington called, "I'll send some cavalry after you as soon as they're ready."

Fetterman acknowledged what he had said and, at a trot, led his command on out through the gate. Paddock wondered where Brown was. He had made a point of being ready in case of just such an eventuality as this and now he was nowhere to be seen.

Staring after Fetterman's command, the uneasiness he had felt so often over the past couple of weeks returned. The 18th Infantry was equipped with obsolete muzzle-loading Springfield rifles. Against the thousands of Indians Paddock knew were waiting for them, they would be virtually helpless. Fifty men, fifty shots. It took several minutes for the troopers to reload the Springfields and the Sioux would not be idle then.

There was considerable shouting on the parade as the cavalry began to form ranks there. Captain Brown came trotting from the stables mounted on Jimmy Carrington's spotted pony Calico, which he had apparently borrowed from the boy. Two civilian employees, Jim Wheatley and Ike Fisher, armed with repeating Henry rifles, joined the cavalry, obviously hoping they would be allowed to go along.

Paddock breathed a little easier when he saw the rifles the cavalrymen were carrying. They were Spencers, seven shot repeaters that had been taken from the Regimental Band a few days earlier and given to them instead.

Lt. Wands, officer of the day, strode swiftly to Carrington. Saluting, he said, "Colonel, Lieutenant Grummond would like to know who is taking out the cavalry."

Carrington smiled but his eyes remained concerned. "I take it Grummond would like to go."

"Yes, *sir.*"

"Then tell him to go ahead, but to report to me before he leaves. And tell him his orders are to join Colonel Fetterman, report to and receive all his orders from Colonel Fetterman. Also he is to tell Colonel Fetterman to remember that his orders were to go out and relieve the wood train, bring it back if necessary, or if he thought best, take the train to the woods and later bring it back. Under no circumstances is he to cross the bluff in pursuit of Indians."

Wands saluted again. "Yes, sir. I will relay those orders to him." He walked quickly away and rejoined Grummond on the far side of the parade.

There were twenty-seven men in the cavalry company, which was Company C, of the Second Cavalry. With Grummond, Brown, Wheatley and Fisher, the total came to thirty-one. With Fetterman and his forty-nine, it made eighty-one men in all. Paddock said, "Want me to go with this bunch, Colonel?" The colonel answered him this time with only an abrupt shake of his head.

He had no faith in Grummond either, Paddock thought, and he was holding Paddock back to carry direct orders to the two commanders if it became apparent they were disobeying the ones he had given them when they left the fort.

Lt. Grummond waved his arm, gave the command to move and cantered out of the fort, with Captain Brown riding beside him on Calico, with Fisher and Wheatley riding just behind. The ponderous gates swung shut and Paddock rode his horse closer to the stockade so that he could better see over the top of it.

He stared in disbelief. Carrington had been justified in thinking his orders would be disobeyed. The colonel suddenly roared at Grummond, just outside the fort. He ran swiftly along the banquette and climbed to the sentry's platform. Grummond halted his command and rode back, halting just below the platform where the Colonel stood.

Carrington repeated the orders he had given Grummond earlier through Lieutenant Wands, and asked if he understood them thoroughly. Grummond nodded somewhat irritably and said he did. He turned and rejoined his command and they galloped after Col. Fetterman. Carrington watched, scowling angrily.

CHAPTER 14

It was obvious, almost from the time that Col. Fetterman left the fort with his fifty mounted infantrymen, that he had no intention whatever of obeying the orders given him by Col. Carrington. The wood train was corralled and fighting the Indians a couple of miles due west of the fort on the south side of the Sullivant Hills. Fetterman headed due north instead of west, straight toward the eastern end of Lodge Trail Ridge, which Carrington had told him specifically not to cross.

Carrington's anger over this deliberate disobedience was just as obvious. His face was red, his eyes narrowed and angry. Paddock rode closer to him and asked, "Want me to try and catch him, Colonel? If he's headed for the wood train, he's sure as hell going at it by a roundabout way."

Carrington hesitated an instant. Then he shook his head. "No. Grummond will catch up and remind him of his orders. He'll turn back."

Paddock didn't say anything but he was

thinking that Grummond wasn't much better than Fetterman as far as obeying orders was concerned. And by the time Carrington found out that neither Fetterman nor Grummond intended to turn back, it would be too late for a messenger to reach them from the fort.

Carrington's eyes were fixed on Fetterman's little force. It had reached Big Piney Creek. There was still time, Paddock thought, for Fetterman to obey the orders given him. He could turn west along the south side of Big Piney Creek and come over the Sullivant Hills behind the Indians.

But Fetterman did not turn. His command splashed across the ice-bordered creek and started up the near slope of Lodge Trail Ridge. Carrington's orders to Fetterman had been "under no circumstances are you to pursue Indians over the ridge" — over Lodge Trail Ridge. Technically, then, Fetterman was not disobeying that part of the orders given him. He was not pursuing anything.

Grummond's cavalry troop, galloping in an effort to catch up, finally caught Fetterman's force just beyond the Big Piney crossing. Both commands halted a moment, and Paddock could see Grummond and Fetterman conferring.

Carrington's face had relaxed somewhat as if he anticipated that both commands would now turn back.

But neither did. Instead, they moved on up the slope of Lodge Trail Ridge. Paddock saw Fetterman wave his hand and the command spread out to left and right as skirmishers as if action with the Indians was imminent.

Carrington said, "Damn!" and turned his head to look at Jess. "At least they're not riding into the Indian trap. Maybe they'll actually be able to come around behind the Indians."

Paddock said, "Won't do 'em any good. A thousand Indians are waiting out there and Fetterman has eighty men. I don't care what side he hits 'em from, eighty men can't beat a thousand."

They still could hear firing from the direction of the besieged wood train. Carrington turned suddenly and yelled. "Lieutenant Wands!"

Wands, who had borrowed a horse somewhere, came trotting to where Carrington stood on the sentry platform. "Yes, sir?"

"Find Dr. Hines. There may be casualties at the wood train and if Fetterman isn't going to relieve it, Hines had better go out there and take care of them."

Lt. Wands asked, "Are you going to send another force to relieve the wood train? Do you want me to get them ready?"

Carrington shook his head. "Not right now. I want to wait and see what Fetterman and Grummond do. Just get Dr. Hines, and a few volunteers to go with him. Three or four will do."

Wands trotted his horse away across the parade toward the post hospital.

Carrington looked at Paddock. "Do you mind going along with Hines?"

"No, Colonel. I'll go." Paddock glanced across the parade toward the post hospital and saw Dr. Hines and his orderly come hurrying out. Hines was carrying his black leather bag. Wands yelled at a couple of mounted infantrymen and they broke out of their formation on the parade and brought their horses to Hines and his orderly. Another man, a civilian named Portugee Phillips, joined the two, as did Sergeant O'Mara. The four came riding across the parade toward Carrington.

It was the first time Paddock had seen O'Mara since the fight and he watched the sergeant warily. Surprisingly, O'Mara grinned at him. "Howdy, Bucko. You goin' along with the surgeon too?"

Paddock nodded, frowning slightly because

O'Mara's sudden change of attitude puzzled him. Maybe the fight had cleared the air, he thought. Maybe by slugging it out with O'Mara until both were on the verge of unconsciousness, he had earned the burly sergeant's respect, something he would probably have been unable to do in any other way.

He shrugged slightly, accepting the change in the man even though he didn't entirely understand it. Briefly he studied O'Mara, trying to decide if the sergeant's new attitude toward him was genuine or feigned. He decided O'Mara was much too direct to feign anything like that.

Carrington said, "Doctor, I want you to ride out to the wood train and treat any wounded they may have. After that is done, Paddock will guide you to Fetterman and Grummond and you are to stay with them."

Hines nodded. "All right, Colonel." He turned his head and looked at the men with him. "Ready?"

Paddock nodded, and Hines headed toward the gate. Carrington was still on the sentry platform, a very worried look upon his face.

The massive gates swung open and the little group rode through. Hines rode in front with Paddock. O'Mara and the doctor's orderly rode immediately behind, followed by Phillips, the civilian.

They were no more than fifty yards from the gate when they heard galloping hoofs behind. Turning his head, Paddock saw Lt. Matson and an infantry private overtaking them. Hines halted long enough for the pair to catch up and then went on. Half a mile farther along the road they overtook a wagon in which were two civilian employees of the quartermaster depot. These had apparently left the fort while everybody's attention was on the troops being readied on the parade. What they had in mind and what they thought they could accomplish was a mystery.

Hines slowed enough for the men with the wagon to keep up. He obviously did not want to leave them behind, alone and exposed to attack by lurking Indians.

Paddock had not seen an Indian since leaving the fort and he was beginning to feel uneasy about it. O'Mara, as though echoing his thoughts, said, "Bejesus, where are all the redskins, Bucko? It's like they'd vanished into the air."

Paddock could no longer hear the sounds of firing from the direction of the corraled wood train. They rounded the knoll that hid the train from the fort and saw it suddenly ahead of them. It was breaking its protective square and heading once more toward the Pinery. There still was not an Indian in sight.

Paddock's mild uneasiness had now changed to deep concern. The fact that the Indians had so suddenly and precipitantly withdrawn could only mean that a trap had indeed been set for Fetterman. As soon as he had left the fort and headed for Lodge Trail Ridge, the Indians must have broken off the engagement with the corraled wood train.

He turned his head. "Want me to ride ahead and see if they've got any casualties, Dr. Hines?"

Hines nodded. Paddock dug spurs into his horse's sides and the animal galloped eagerly along the rutted road, which now began to climb the divide between the two branches of Piney Creek. O'Mara, surprisingly, joined him before he had gone a hundred yards.

The wood train was more than a mile ahead and had almost reached the bridge Carrington had built across Big Piney Creek before Paddock and O'Mara were able to catch up with it. Corporal LeGrow was riding in the rear wagon and O'Mara yelled at him, "You got any casualties, Corporal?"

LeGrow shook his head. "Nothin' serious. One of the teamsters got an arrow through his shoulder, but I pulled it out. He's still drivin' to keep from gettin' stiff."

"You don't need the doctor then?"

"Hell no. We're goin' on to the Pinery to get a load of logs."

O'Mara nodded and stopped his horse. The two watched the wood train cross the bridge. It wound up the steep and twisting road into the pines. O'Mara said, "Bucko, it looks like Colonel Fetterman has bit off more than he can chew."

Paddock had been thinking the same thing. He cocked his head and listened intently for the sound of firing from the direction Fetterman had gone. All he heard was the murmur of the stream and the wind whispering through the pines. He said, "Let's get back to Dr. Hines."

He did not gallop his horse going back because he knew that before he returned to the fort he might need every bit of strength and stamina the horse possessed. He was becoming increasingly uneasy about Fetterman and his eighty men, and the silence was anything but reassuring. The Indians were probably only waiting until

Fetterman's men got far enough away from the fort so that rescue was impossible.

O'Mara asked, "You don't think Fetterman is going to try attacking their villages on the Tongue, do you? I've heard him say he could ride through the whole Sioux nation with a hundred men."

Paddock didn't know. Fetterman had certainly headed away from the fort as if he knew exactly where he was going. He said, "I don't think even Fetterman could be that stupid. Fifty of his men are armed with those damned muzzle-loading Springfields."

"Then where the hell *has* he gone? If he intended to circle around and hit the bucks that was attackin' the wood train, he'd have been here by now."

Involuntarily Paddock glanced up toward the crest of the Sullivant Hills. He saw no movement there.

Fetterman had disobeyed his orders. He had gone over Lodge Trail Ridge, taking Grummond along with him. He'd never had any intention of coming to the wood train's relief, and that fact must be plain to Col. Carrington by now. Paddock wondered what Carrington would do. Would he send out another force to relieve Fetterman? Or would he wait to see if Fetterman made it safely back?

Shrugging fatalistically, he kicked his horse

into a trot, and ten minutes later reached Dr. Hines and the other men. He said, "They only have one casualty, Doctor, a man with an arrow through his shoulder. Corporal LeGrow pulled it out and he says the man is driving to keep it from getting stiff."

"Then they don't need me."

"No. I guess we'd better see if we can find Colonel Fetterman."

Hines nodded. He turned to the men in the wagon. "Take your choice. Drive on and join the wood train or go back to the fort. We're heading over the hill and we can't take you along."

The driver, his face bearded and seamed, said, "We'll join the wood train, I reckon."

Hines nodded, and looked at Lt. Matson and the infantryman. "You can come along or go back to the fort."

Matson said, "We'll stay with you."

"Then let's get on with it. Paddock, lead the way."

Paddock put his horse up the steep slope, heading for a narrow ravine between two rounded hills. The others spurred their horses after his, the animals lunging because of the steepness of the trail.

And now, so faintly he could not be sure of it, Paddock thought he heard firing from ahead.

CHAPTER 15

At this moment, they were about three miles from the fort. Looking east, Paddock could see it, but the distance was too great to make out individual figures inside its walls. He wondered if Carrington had done anything about sending a relief force after Fetterman. He doubted it. Fetterman had eighty men and there were ninety with the wood train. Carrington could not have much more than two hundred left at the fort. He would think twice about sending any substantial force to Fetterman's relief because doing so would leave the fort itself dangerously undermanned.

Halfway up the south side of the Sullivant Hills, Paddock halted to let the horses blow. They fidgeted, tossing their heads and rattling their bits. Paddock kept an ear cocked toward the north, listening for the sounds of firing. This time he was sure he heard it even though the distance was considerable and even though two ridges lay between him and Fetterman's men. Dr. Hines said, "That's gunfire all right. No doubt of it."

Paddock nodded. The horses' breathing was more regular now and he touched spurs to his horse's sides. The animal lunged on up the steep slope toward the top of the ridge.

Reaching it, Paddock halted again. The firing was now very distinct but Fetterman's force was nowhere to be seen. The sounds seemed to be coming from a spot perhaps two and a half miles to the northeast. Paddock urged his horse down the northern side of the Sullivant Hills toward Big Piney Creek in the valley below. The going was treacherous and several times his horse slid on his haunches. When he reached the bottom, his legs were trembling.

The others slid their horses down behind Paddock and halted beside him. Here, Big Piney Creek ran narrow and deep and very swift, its banks steep and overgrown with brush and trees. Hines said, "Let's go downstream a ways and see if we can't find a better place to cross."

Paddock nodded. He put his horse into a trot, paralleling Big Piney Creek. There was no advantage in trying to cross it here. Doing so would neither save time nor shorten greatly the distance to Fetterman and his men. They still would have to cross Lodge Trail Ridge, descend into a ravine, and climb the ridge beyond. If they followed Big Piney Creek to the regular crossing of the Bozeman Road, they could then follow the road north on an easy grade, gaining time and saving the horses as well.

O'Mara ranged his horse up beside Paddock's. There was worry in the sergeant's eyes. "What do you think, Bucko? You think Fetterman's in trouble?"

Paddock nodded. "There are at least a thousand Indians out there and maybe more."

O'Mara said, "He claimed he could ride through them with a hundred men. Looks like he's got his chance."

"Don't like him much, do you?"

O'Mara looked surprised. Frowning, he thought about it and finally said, "I guess I don't, now you mention it. To him, them troopers are only tools. And that damned Brown is worse. He's so hot to have an Indian scalp he'd sacrifice his own mother to get one. No, I guess I ain't got much use for either one of 'em."

The firing continued as they rode. Paddock kept watch for a crossing but did not find one until they reached the place where the Bozeman Road crossed the creek.

By now, the hills to the north were swarming with Indians. They galloped back and forth with seeming aimlessness, like ants in an anthill that has been disturbed. Hines stared northward worriedly. "What do you think, Jess? Can we get through?"

Hines continued to stare north along the climbing course of the Bozeman Road. At last he said, "Fetterman is probably surrounded, and if he is, we haven't got a chance of reaching him. At least not without reinforcements."

Paddock nodded. "You may be right. Why don't you and Lt. Matson go back to the fort and get more men? Fetterman likely needs help more than he needs you."

Hines nodded and turned to go. Looking back he said, "You sounded like you weren't going along with us. What are *you* going to do?"

"Fetterman's force may still be intact. I thought I'd try reaching him to tell him Carrington wants him to turn back. Maybe it's not too late. There's still a lot of firing over there and we know the Indians don't have many guns. So most of Fetterman's men must still be all right."

Hines touched heels to his horse's sides and the animal trotted away. Lt. Matson and the infantryman fell in behind, as did

Phillips, the civilian. O'Mara hesitated. He looked after the doctor, then back to Paddock. At last he asked, "Mind if I go with you?"

Paddock shook his head. "I don't mind, but you might lose your hair."

"You think you're any better than me?"

Paddock said, "Oh Christ, let's don't start that again."

O'Mara grinned unexpectedly.

Paddock studied the man with something like regret. He knew that his decision to try reaching Fetterman had been brash and ill-considered. There was little chance they could reach Fetterman and even if they did, little chance that Fetterman, having initially disobeyed Carrington's orders, would now heed them and turn back to the fort. But he'd stuck his neck out and he had to go through with it.

He stared up the Bozeman Road once more. He could, at any given time, count thirty or forty Indians galloping back and forth across it near the top of the ridge. He wondered how far Fetterman and Brown had gone before the Indians had pinned them down. The firing now seemed to be stationary. Fetterman's infantry and Grummond's cavalry must have taken cover on some hillside and be fighting it out even though completely surrounded by the Indians. Still, Fetterman and Brown had successfully fought their way through several hundred Indians on December 6th. If Hines brought out a relief force Fetterman still might be extricated from the situation with little loss.

He beckoned to O'Mara, then ascended through the timber on the east side of the ridge. This way, perhaps they could avoid discovery at least until they were a quarter to a half mile away. It was slower going but the Bozeman Road was too open and exposed.

Behind him, O'Mara said, "I must be crazy for offering to go with you."

Paddock grinned. "And I'm crazy for going."

"Do you really think we can get through?"

Paddock shook his head. "No, I never did think we could."

"Then what the hell are we doing here?"

"I want to find out how much trouble Fetterman is in. I want to be able to tell Colonel Carrington how many men are going to be needed to get him out of it."

O'Mara looked relieved. "Well, I'm glad you're not going to try riding through all them howlin' devils. How close do you think we'll have to get?"

Paddock shrugged. "Close enough to

see what's going on."

A mile from the creek, Paddock drew rein in a thick grove of pines. They were closer to the firing now, which had continued unabated. If there had been any doubt before about the seriousness of Fetterman's predicament, none remained. He had apparently been pinned down at least half an hour, maybe longer. His men were fighting for their lives.

Conscious that little time now remained, Paddock spurred his horse suddenly, and recklessly climbed to the Bozeman Road on the spine of the ridge. Pounding along beside him, O'Mara yelled, "Have you lost your mind? What are you trying to do?"

"Find out what's going on before it's too late. They must be getting low on ammunition. They've been firing for more than half an hour now."

O'Mara looked at him and shook his head. He dropped back a little but he kept pace. Paddock reached a spot near the crest of the ridge and from here could see far enough ahead to grasp the scope of the Indian attack.

Involuntarily he pulled his horse to a halt. It was hard to estimate a rapidly moving, close-packed body of Indians, but it looked to him as though there must be twice as many involved in this attack on Fetterman as he had seen rehearsing their trap several days before. He and O'Mara did not seem to have been spotted, even though they now were less than half a mile from the nearest Indians. O'Mara yelled, "For Christ's sake, let's get back to the fort. Fetterman needs help and needs it bad."

Paddock yelled, "You go on back. Tell Carrington to send out some men. And some artillery. That's what it'll take to scatter that bunch."

O'Mara shook his head. "I'm not going back until you do, Bucko."

"Don't be a fool!"

O'Mara grinned. "You mean don't be like you?" Paddock shrugged. He touched his horse's sides with his spurs and the animal, seemingly infected with his rider's excitement, pounded up the rutted, narrow road.

CHAPTER 16

Not long afterward, Paddock and O'Mara reached a high point from which they could clearly see ahead. Now, for the first time, Paddock saw the blue uniforms of Fetterman's infantrymen and those of Grummond's cavalry, half a mile ahead.

It was obvious that Fetterman's command had been spread out as skirmishers but under the unrelenting pressure of the howling, circling Indians, the skirmishers farthest out had been forced back in toward the center of the line.

Slow progress by both commands had led Paddock to believe the racket of firing was stationary while actually it was not. Both Fetterman and Grummond had apparently continued to move in much the same way Fetterman had on December 6th, slowly, almost inch by inch through the ever closing circle of Indians.

Mindful of the experience on December 4th, when Bingham had lost his head and retreated from that pressure, Fetterman had made no attempt to turn back or retreat toward the fort, but instead had continued stubbornly to go ahead. Whether that was right or not was problematical. Retreating would have given the Indians the idea that they had the white soldiers on the run. Continuing to advance when there was no place to go might turn out to be as disastrous as the first course would have been.

Quite obviously, Fetterman was holding his men together only by the sheer force of his own will. They were firing raggedly, and, with the ancient muzzle-loading Springfields, were forced after each shot to stop, to ram home a charge, to follow it with a ball, and then, before they could fire again, to affix a cap. The whole reloading process could not be done, even by an expert, in less than a minute and none of Fetterman's men were expert. Reloading usually took from three to five minutes and during that time the soldier was helpless, unable to defend himself.

There were some casualties, but from this distance it was hard to tell how many or how serious they were. Fetterman's men would be reluctant to leave their dead behind because they knew how horribly the bodies would be mutilated by the Indians. Paddock supposed some of those being dragged or carried along with the command were already dead.

He thought Fetterman must know that he was doomed. The men must also know. Looking beyond Fetterman's command, he could see Grummond's cavalry. Like Fetterman's men, they had dismounted to fight on foot, turning the horses over to horse holders. The horses were in the center of the circle they had formed, the cavalrymen forming its perimeter. They were better able to keep the Indians at a distance with their repeating Spencers and seemed in no immediate danger.

Silently, Paddock exhorted Grummond to turn back and help Fetterman. The colonel was in dire need right now of more firepower, firepower that could be supplied by Grummond's cavalry. But Grummond apparently was not aware of Fetterman's need and made no attempt to return and help him out.

He saw a man fall on Fetterman's right flank, and another, and another still, and so close was the horde of Indians that their bodies could not be recovered by their comrades before they were swarmed over by the Sioux. Uniforms were snatched off, to reappear almost at once on the bodies of the Indians, a hat on one, a tunic on another, a pair of trousers on a third. A glimpse through the milling Indians showed Paddock a gleam of white, which must have been the naked body of one of the dead infantrymen.

He realized that he had been watching in a kind of a daze. He turned his head and looked at Sergeant O'Mara. He wondered if his own face was as white as O'Mara's was. He yelled, "Get back to the fort. Tell the colonel what's going on."

"What are you going to do?"

"I'm going to try and reach Grummond. If he doesn't get back to Fetterman and help him out, Fetterman's men are dead."

"You can't get through that bunch of Indians!"

"I'm going to try."

"You're a damned fool!"

"Probably. Get going. Tell Carrington to get some howitzers out here as fast as he can."

O'Mara shook his head. "Dr. Hines has already told him that. I'm going with you, Bucko. If you're going to make a jackass out of yourself, then I'd just as well do it too."

Paddock didn't have time to argue the point with him. Besides, he knew O'Mara probably was right. Hines and Lt. Matson had gone back to the fort earlier. A relief force should already be on its way and Col. Carrington would not have to be told to send artillery along. It was the only thing the Indians feared.

He dug spurs into his horse's sides and the startled animal leaped ahead. He couldn't help thinking about Molly Benedict and for an instant he could see, in his mind, her white face looking at him from the crowd beside the stockade gate. He remembered the way her lips had been parted and the terror in her eyes. And he wondered if he would ever see her again.

He leaned low over his horse's withers, drawing his revolver as he did. He could hear the thunder of O'Mara's horse pounding along behind. Fetterman's men seemed to have come to a halt. The last of the skirmishers had joined the main command, which now was huddled so closely together that Paddock wondered how they could even fight.

He thought savagely, "Spread out, you damn fools! Spread out and take cover! You're just making it easy for them to kill you off!"

But the men of Fetterman's command were thoroughly demoralized by the awful pressure of the Indians. And they knew there was no way of getting out of this alive. The fort was miles away and more than a thousand Indians barred their way to it. They knew death was very close.

Paddock could no longer see Fetterman. He wondered if the colonel had been killed. Perhaps he had. It would explain the thorough demoralization of his men.

Now, less than a quarter mile separated Paddock and O'Mara from Fetterman's mauled command. And suddenly, for the first time, they were spotted by the Indians.

The howling quieted. A couple of hundred of the Indians nearest them halted their ponies and milled about uncertainly, staring down the road past Paddock and O'Mara as though they believed they were the vanguard of a relief force from the fort. But when they saw no soldiers coming on behind the pair, they began to howl again, even louder than before. A body of at least two hundred detached itself from the others and came galloping down the Bozeman Road straight toward the two.

O'Mara yelled, "Holy Christ! We'll never get through now."

Paddock knew there had probably never been the slightest chance of getting through. It had been a foolish idea and now they could just as well give it up.

He glanced past the rapidly approaching Indians, beyond Fetterman's huddled command, to that of Grummond farther on which still seemed to be intact, but would not be long. As soon as the Indians had killed the last of Fetterman's command, they would turn to Grummond's and annihilate it too. He caught a glimpse of a spotted horse. Jimmy Carrington's horse, he thought, the one Brown had borrowed so that he could go after the Indian scalp he had talked so much about.

He hauled his horse in so abruptly that the animal reared, pawing the air and fighting for his head. O'Mara's horse came to a stiff-legged halt immediately behind, then whirled and began to buck. The sergeant stayed with him for half a dozen jumps, fighting to yank up his head, cursing savagely all the while. Then suddenly O'Mara sailed off, striking the dirt of the road with a thud and skidding half a dozen feet.

Paddock didn't even look at him. He spurred, and reined his horse hard over toward O'Mara's, now galloping down through the thick timber on the east side of the ridge.

Almost immediately he realized that he couldn't overtake the horse in time to return him to O'Mara before he was overrun by Indians. He therefore abandoned his attempt to catch the horse and returned at a gallop to where O'Mara lay.

The fall had driven the air from O'Mara's lungs. He lay on his side in a crouched position, fighting desperately for breath. Paddock roared, "O'Mara! Get up behind me! Quick!"

O'Mara glanced up, his face dirty and almost green. His eyes showed his agony. It was with a superhuman effort that he fought to his hands and knees.

The Sioux were closer now and their howls made O'Mara turn his head. The Indians were galloping along the crest of the ridge about ten abreast, a solid wall of barbaric fury the sight of which brought O'Mara stumbling to his feet. He caught Paddock's saddle horn and slammed a foot into the stirrup Paddock gave to him. The horse was already running as he hit its back behind Paddock's saddle. He held on by putting his arms around Paddock while he continued to fight desperately for breath.

An arrow whistled past Paddock's head and struck the road a dozen feet ahead. Another scratched the horse's rump, bringing blood but falling to the road.

The pain made the horse run even faster than before. But he was carrying double weight and could not possibly outrun the Indians. It was only a matter of time before they got close enough to knock both Paddock and O'Mara out of the saddle.

Paddock heard the solid thump of the arrow that struck Sergeant O'Mara in the back. And he felt the way O'Mara's arms tightened briefly before they fell away.

O'Mara sagged to the right, dead weight, and Paddock half turned in the saddle, holding him, keeping him from falling off. Immediately ahead there was a cluster of rocks beside the road. He turned slightly, reining in. The horse showed its side to the pursuing Indians, and took an arrow in the neck.

He went down, throwing both Paddock and O'Mara neatly over his head. Rolling and skidding in a cloud of dust, the pair, with O'Mara wholly limp, rolled into the shelter of the rocks. The horse somersaulted once and then lay still, forming a bulwark between Paddock and the Indians, who now were hauling their horses to a halt and milling in confusion less than thirty yards away.

Paddock's revolver still was in his hand. He fired carefully, and with three shots knocked three Indians from their saddles. The others split to right and left, bent on encircling the rocks. He took advantage of the brief respite to look at O'Mara and to grasp his wrist. There was no pulse and O'Mara's chest was still. The arrow must have pierced his heart and killed him instantly.

Turning, Paddock fired twice more, then crouched behind his horse and replaced the spent cylinder with a loaded one. Arrows thudded into the horse and into the ground immediately behind. They made an unmistakable twanging sound as they left the bow, and an equally unmistakable thud as they struck.

Paddock yanked his rifle from the saddle boot and laid it beside him against the time when the revolver would be empty again.

He thought, "God damn it, I'm not going to get out of this," and reared up to fire at two Indians, running toward him half crouched, one carrying a knife, the other a tomahawk. He killed the one with the knife with a bullet in the chest and, firing hastily, broke the leg of the second one.

Behind them, three more Indians came galloping, intending to run him down or flush him out for the other Indians, now ranged on both sides and behind the cluster of rocks.

Paddock rammed his revolver back into its holster and snatched up his rifle before he leaped aside. He set himself and, standing spread-legged, swung the rifle like a club.

It struck the nearest Indian in the chest, forcing an explosive grunt out of him, driving him backward over his horse's rump. The horse, confused and terrified, reared and turned, pawing the air over Paddock's head. Paddock had a quick glimpse of the painted faces of the other two Indians as they went past and then he knew this rearing horse was the only chance he was going to get to stay alive. He ducked the flailing hoofs and as the horse came down, seized its bridle on the left side of its head.

His strange smell further terrified the horse. He whirled, and plunged away, dragging Paddock along with him. Using the horse's speed and the leverage his grip on the bridle gave him, Paddock swung to the horse's back, forced to release his rifle as he did so that he could grasp the horse's mane. Mounted, he leaned far forward and caught up the dragging reins before the horse broke them by stepping on them.

Everything had happened so quickly he didn't know which way he was headed and he was relieved to realize he was headed down the Bozeman Road toward the fort.

Once more the Indians were in full and howling pursuit. But about half of them had stayed behind to strip and mutilate the body of the dead O'Mara.

Paddock found it hard to believe that he was alive. He had faced certain death there in the rocks but he had not died. Now he faced life again, finding it unbelievably sweet. He raked the terrified Indian pony with his spurs, leaning low and riding as he had never ridden in his life before.

CHAPTER 17

What had started out this morning as a routine situation, with the wood train going out, being attacked and promptly being relieved had turned into a nightmare because of one officer's insubordination. Paddock now knew that Fetterman's whole command was doomed. Grummond's cavalry, or part of it, might be saved, but only if they were reached immediately.

The stocky Indian pony was thoroughly terrified by the strange smell of his rider and ran willingly. Arrows whizzed past Paddock's head, falling to the ground in the road ahead of him. Glancing back, he saw that the pursuing Indians were less than fifty yards behind. He considered using his revolver to discourage them but gave the idea up. He only had three loads left and he might need them desperately later on.

Half a mile fell behind, a mile. And then, ahead, Paddock saw the blue uniforms of a relief force coming up the road. They were almost all on foot, but moving at double time. They appeared to be about forty of them in all. Two ambulances followed them. Paddock kept his Indian pony at a run until he was within a hundred yards of the column's head. Glancing behind as he hauled the pony to a halt, he discovered that the Indians had given up the chase. They now were trotting their ponies back up the road.

He released a long sigh of relief. He discovered, when he dismounted, that his knees were trembling so badly he could hardly stand. He grinned shakily at Captain Ten Eyck, commander of the relief column. "Godalmighty, that was close!"

Ten Eyck did not stop, but continued to double time swiftly up the road, motioning for Paddock to keep pace with him. The Indian pony, frightened by the men coming behind Captain Ten Eyck, permitted Paddock to lead him. Ten Eyck asked, "What's going on, Jess?"

"Fetterman's in trouble. He may be dead and by the time we get there all his men may be dead too."

"Fifty men?" Ten Eyck's tone was incredulous.

Paddock nodded. "Grummond and his cavalry were in fair shape the last I saw of them because of the Spencer rifles they were carrying, but as soon as the Indians finish Fetterman off, they'll turn on Grummond and his men."

"What do you think we ought to do?"

"Keep going, but don't go into anything blind. Have you got artillery?"

Ten Eyck shook his head.

"Then I'd suggest you send someone back to the fort for two or three howitzers. Artillery is the one thing those Indians fear."

Ten Eyck turned his head and yelled at a mounted civilian riding just ahead of the wagons. The man, bearded and graying, trotted his horse forward. "Yeah, Captain?"

"Ride back to the fort as fast as you can. Tell Colonel Carrington I'm going to need some artillery and if he can spare them, some more men too." He turned his head and spoke to his orderly, "Private Sample, you go with him. Borrow a horse from somebody."

The two men galloped back down the road. The fort was still visible from here and Paddock thought they could have saved time with a heliograph if the sun had not been hidden behind gray and heavy clouds.

He saw Dr. Hines with the column of men behind Ten Eyck, and Lt. Matson too.

Hines called to him, "Where's Sergeant O'Mara, Jess?"

Paddock waited for part of the column to pass. Abreast of Dr. Hines, he said, "Dead. His horse bucked him off and ran away. He got up behind me and caught an arrow in the back."

"What happened to your horse?"

"Arrow in the neck. I borrowed an Indian horse."

Paddock mounted, left Dr. Hines and rode his Indian pony once more to the column's head. Captain Ten Eyck was plainly nervous and searched the timber on both sides of him with worried eyes. He glanced at Paddock and asked, "How many Indians did you say there were?"

Paddock said, "I don't know, Captain. It's hard to count when you're trying to stay alive. But I'd guess somewhere between fifteen hundred and two thousand."

"How were they armed?"

"Mostly with bows and arrows and spears and tomahawks. But they've likely got all of Fetterman's Springfields, now, and maybe Grummond's Spencers too."

Ten Eyck nodded, his eyes preoccupied. He was plainly concerned about the safety of his command. Fetterman had ridden into a trap and had seen his men slaughtered.

Ten Eyck didn't intend to let that happen to him if ordinary prudence could prevent it.

The road continued to ascend and, about a mile from where he had encountered Paddock, Ten Eyck ordered his command to veer right toward a high promontory from which he could better see the land ahead.

Paddock watched approvingly. Obviously Ten Eyck was not the firebrand that Fetterman and Brown were. Ten Eyck was trying to do what he had been ordered to do, relieve Fetterman's command, but he was also trying to avoid walking into the same kind of trap. He didn't have the mobility Fetterman and Grummond had, since his command was on foot, and he didn't have as many men. He was painfully aware that the Indians, having killed all of both Fetterman's and Grummond's commands would probably turn on him.

The men plodded through the timber, ascending to the rocky point. Ten Eyck had earlier ordered flankers out to guard against surprise attack. Reaching the promontory, he halted and stared at the land ahead.

Even from this high promontory, it still was not possible to see the slope where

Fetterman's men were engaged, nor the place farther on to which Grummond's cavalry had advanced. The firing, furthermore, had all but ceased.

Ten Eyck glanced up at Paddock. "See anything?"

"Just Indians milling around."

"Nothing of Fetterman?"

Paddock shook his head.

The Indians covered the crest of the ridge between where Ten Eyck had halted and the place where Paddock had last seen Fetterman. They seemed to be milling around aimlessly, as though uncertain as to what they ought to do.

The halt took no more than a few minutes but it accomplished its main purpose. Ten Eyck was able to see into a deep ravine lying to the right of the road and to satisfy himself that no Indians waited there to ambush him. Having done so, he gave the order to advance. He proceeded back to the road and then along it to the place where it began its descent into Peno Creek.

From here, the road dropped abruptly for about half a mile, then continued to descend more gradually for another half mile. From that point the road followed a narrow ridge for almost a mile and then dropped off abruptly into the valley of Peno Creek. At both ends of the narrow ridge were numbers of large rocks lying beside the road. Paddock was looking at the place he had last seen Fetterman but right now he couldn't see anything except the Indians milling around the nearest pile of rocks. It was an eerie experience. It was almost as though he had imagined what he had seen earlier, as though Fetterman's command, and Grummond's, had vanished from the face of the earth.

The column moved down the descending road, the ambulances creaking along in the rear. Paddock watched the Indians retreat before them, and realized that the Sioux thought the two ambulances contained artillery. He said, "They think we've got howitzers in the wagons, Captain."

"Then let's hope they keep on thinking so."

While they were still half a mile from the place where he had last seen Fetterman, Paddock caught a glimpse of something white. An instant later, he saw several more white spots, and realized that they were bodies, stripped and lying on the ground. He said. "Captain, I see bodies up there near the rocks."

"How many? Can you tell?" Ten Eyck's

eyes were narrowed and he was staring ahead, but he did not have the advantage of being on a horse.

Paddock now could make out a large number of naked bodies, but because of the distance it was impossible to make a count. He said, "A lot of them, Captain. A hell of a lot of them."

Ten Eyck said in a shocked voice, "Oh God! I can see them now myself. Aren't there any left alive?"

"I don't see anything but bodies, Captain."

There still were a number of Indians among the bodies and Ten Eyck ordered angrily, "Spread out and open fire! Drive those damned vultures out of there!"

The men behind him spread to right and left, knelt and opened fire. The Indians milling around among the bodies mounted immediately and galloped away down the road, not stopping until they were out of range.

Ten Eyck yelled, "Cease firing!" and the firing stopped. Paddock heard the rattling of tug chains and the creak of wagon wheels and, looking back, saw three wagons, an ambulance and about forty civilians coming down the road from the direction of the fort. Some of the men were on foot, but most were mounted. All were armed heavily.

Paddock glanced at Ten Eyck's face. It showed his relief at being thus reinforced. Ahead and well beyond the place where the bodies were, the Sioux seemed to be forming ranks again, perhaps for another attack upon the hated whites.

On down the road the reinforced column went. The faces of the men were white with shock, but here and there was a red and angry face. From the direction of the fort came Private Sample, galloping his horse. He reined up beside Captain Ten Eyck, dismounted and handed him a piece of paper. Ten Eyck read it as he marched, his face emotionless. Turning, he handed the paper to Paddock.

It was hastily scrawled and the paper was rumpled, but it was easy enough to read. It said, "Captain: Forty well-armed men with 3000 rounds, ambulances, etc., left before your courier came in. You must unite with Fetterman; fire slowly and keep men in hand; you would have saved two miles toward scene of action if you had taken Lodge Trail Ridge. I ordered the wood train in, which will give fifty more men to spare."

Ten Eyck said, as though trying to justify himself, "I came by the road because it was quicker and easier on the men and because there was no deep snow. And you know why I rode to that high point, Jess."

Paddock handed the paper back. "I know, Captain, and so does Col. Carrington. He was worried when he wrote this note. He'll be the first to say you did the right thing when he has all the facts."

Ten Eyck shrugged. "I hope so," he said.

They reached the first cluster of rocks at the near end of the ridge and from here they could see the entire battlefield. Nothing alive on the slope to the east of the ridge. It was strewn with the white and naked bodies of the men that had been with Fetterman. All were bristling with arrows, shot into them after they had been stripped. Captain Ten Eyck breathed, "Holy God!"

Paddock felt a little sick himself. An hour ago, these fifty men had been alive. They had headed out of the fort on a routine mission that had been safely accomplished dozens of times in the last few months.

Now, because of Fetterman's ambition and disobedience, they were dead. He let his eyes go past these bodies toward the far end of the ridge. Halfway there he saw more bodies and knew they were Grummond's men.

A few dead horses lay among the bodies

of the slain troopers but most of the horses had disappeared. So had the soldiers' uniforms and so had their guns. There appeared to be forty or fifty bodies in an area that could not have been more than thirty or forty feet in diameter. All were savagely mutilated. In almost all cases, the men's genitals had been cut off and placed inside their mouths, a final indignity that signified both the Indians' hatred and their contempt.

Ten Eyck yelled, his voice coming out thin and strained. "Draw the wagons up here and begin loading the bodies. Keep your guns close at hand." He moved on down the ridge, followed by Paddock and two or three of his men.

Farther down the ridge, they came upon Lt. Grummond's naked body lying in the road. Off to the side, the slope was strewn with the bodies of his men, stripped and mutilated as those of Fetterman's men had been. The only living thing was a wounded horse, which one of the men dispatched with a bullet in the head.

Strangely, one body had been neither mutilated nor stripped. It was that of the bugler, Adolf Metzger. He lay on his back, fully clothed and covered with a buffalo robe. In his hand he still had the bugle, but it now was twisted and bent almost beyond recognition, and it was stained with the blood of the Indians he had clubbed with it.

Ten Eyck stared at the bugler's body. His face was almost gray and there was a film of sweat on it. He looked at Paddock and asked, "What in God's name do you make of that?"

Paddock said, "Indians respect courage above all else. Metzger must have been a tiger. I don't suppose he had a gun, but that didn't slow *him* down. He attacked the Indians with his bugle and he may even have killed one or two of them with it. He'd have to have put on a pretty impressive show to get this kind of respect from the Sioux."

Ten Eyck nodded numbly. Paddock found the bodies of Jim Wheatley and Ike Fisher in some rocks nearby.

Eighty-one men had died for one's man's stubbornness and stupidity. And he thought, "What an awful Goddamned waste!"

CHAPTER 18

Gathering up the bodies of the slaughtered troopers was not a pleasant task. The faces of the men working at it were white with shock. Every now and then a young trooper would run to a nearby clump of brush, there to bend double and throw up, sometimes gagging afterward for a long time before he could return, sweating, to the job.

Ten Eyck organized the men into two shifts, recognizing that no man can work at this kind of grisly task without respite no matter how tough and hardened he might be. Each shift would work for half an hour and then would be relieved by the other shift. Those not working stood guard against the possibility of attack by the Indians, who still were massed a mile away in the valley of Peno Creek.

It was now mid-afternoon. The Indians showed no inclination to attack, no doubt believing that this detachment of soldiers had artillery, but neither did they leave the area.

Paddock found it hard to believe that he

was alive. He knew that only a miracle could have kept him from being killed when O'Mara was. And it was a kind of miracle that he had not been with Fetterman or with Grummond. He had volunteered to go with Fetterman and later with Grummond and had been refused both times.

There were six wagons in all. Each wagon would hold no more than eight men unless Captain Ten Eyck was willing to pile the bodies on top of each other like cordwood. He was not. Obviously he felt these men had suffered enough indignity at the hands of the Indians. He would not add to it.

It was late afternoon by the time all the wagons were loaded and still nearly half of Fetterman's men lay where they had died. Regretfully Ten Eyck gave the order to return to the fort.

Half the command preceded the six wagons; about half came along behind. Ten Eyck rode at the column's head on a horse someone had given him, with Lt. Matson and Dr. Hines. Paddock rode just behind the three with one of the civilian quartermaster department employees.

Nobody talked. The only sounds were those of the horses' hoofs on the frozen road, of the wagon wheels, of the clank of tug chains and singletrees, of the slogging boots of the foot soldiers, some of whom held onto the stirrups of the mounted men to make the going easier.

They brought the fort into sight while yet three miles away, and Paddock could see men lining the stockade, standing on the banquette inside. Only their heads were visible above the pointed stockade posts.

They splashed across Big Piney Creek as the sun sank below the Big Horn Mountains in the west, those on foot not even caring now if they got wet. The wood train, loaded with logs, was arriving from the Pinery as they went through the gates. The men with the wood train seemed to know there had been a battle. They did not know how disastrous it had been until they saw the six wagon loads of bodies entering the fort.

Molly Benedict's was the first face that Paddock saw. He dismounted from the frightened Indian pony and, holding the reins, hugged her close to him. Her face was white, her eyes wide with shock as she asked, "All of them?"

He nodded. "All of them. About thirty are still out there."

He stood with her and watched the six wagons cross the parade to the post hospital. He saw Colonel Carrington talking with Captain Ten Eyck and Dr. Hines. Men came running from the barracks, and Carrington detailed twenty-five or thirty of them to carry the bodies of the dead inside. Hines and his orderlies would remove the arrows and prepare the bodies for burial. The carpenters would be busy all night building coffins out of rough-sawed pine.

Paddock walked beside Molly across the corner of the parade. He left her at the stable long enough to turn his captured Indian pony into the corral. Returning, he walked with her in the gathering darkness toward her house.

They went inside and she lighted the lamp. Silently she brought him a brown bottle of whisky, seeming to know he needed this. He poured a tumbler full and drank it down as if it were water.

He stared at the bottle, wondering how long it would be before he stopped seeing those scattered, naked, arrow-filled and mutilated bodies in his mind. He had fought in the war and had seen dead men before, but there is something that is different about a man's body when it has been deliberately desecrated by his enemy.

He refilled his glass. Molly seemed to know from looking at his face and into his stricken eyes that he didn't want to talk. She sat across the table and waited patiently until he looked at her. Then she asked, "Do you want anything to eat?"

Dumbly he shook his head. He gulped the second glass of whisky but it seemed to have no effect on him. At last Molly asked, "Sergeant O'Mara?"

"Dead. I don't know what the Indians did with his body but it was gone when we came by the place tonight." He poured his glass full for the third time and sat there staring at it. Suddenly he began to shake. It started in his knees and crept over the rest of him until he was shaking from head to foot. His teeth were chattering so badly he couldn't speak.

Tears welled from Molly's eyes. She got up and put some more wood into the stove. She put on the coffeepot and it began to make its peculiar singing sound as it heated.

The shaking lasted five or ten minutes and then it stopped as suddenly as it had begun. Paddock gulped the third glass of whisky. He was beginning to feel a kind of numbness and he supposed that now he probably could sleep. He got wearily to his feet. "I'm going back to my place and sleep."

She didn't protest. She only nodded silently. He knew she was wondering what would happen tomorrow and so said, "I think it's over unless the Indians attack the fort and I don't think they will. Nobody's going out looking for trouble with the Indians after this."

Relief was apparent in her face. He bent his head and kissed her lightly on the mouth. Then he went out.

The wind had begun to blow, an icy wind off the snows of the Big Horn Mountains a dozen miles to the west. It chilled him and he began to shake again. Head down, he hurried to his quarters and went inside.

He built up the fire. Still he felt little effect from the whisky he had drunk. He found a half-filled bottle and took a long drink from it. He stood as close to the stove as he could get. When he finally got warm, he added more wood, closed the damper, and got out of his clothes. He blew out the lamp and, in his underwear, got into bed.

He had been afraid he wouldn't sleep, but he did, almost instantly. It was not, however, a restful sleep. He was tormented with nightmares, not of the battle or of the bodies, but of vague and disconnected things which nevertheless were frightening. Only one thing stood out plainly from all the rest. Someone kept shouting over and over, "I can ride through them with a hundred men! I can ride through them with a hundred men!"

He awoke at dawn and though the room was cold, his body was soaked with sweat. He heard the bugle sounding reveille and he thought about Bugler Metzger, who had fought so ferociously yesterday. He wondered who was taking his place today.

The wind was howling around the eaves. It rattled the door and, when he built a fire, made it roar inside the stove.

He went to the window and stared outside. The Big Horn Mountains were hidden by swirling clouds. He dressed hastily, then took time to carefully reload his revolver cylinders.

When he stepped outside, he could feel the bitter cold. A storm was blowing in. He thought of the more than thirty bodies still lying out there on the hillside four or five miles from the fort. They would be frozen now. Frozen in the positions they had assumed when death caught up with them.

Paddock hurried to the teamsters' mess

and ate for the first time since yesterday morning. Everybody was subdued and there was little talk. There was an air of foreboding in all the men as if they wondered what would happen next.

Outside, Paddock noticed that the sentries had been doubled on all the sentry posts. Carrington obviously thought the fort might be attacked. The Sioux had thoroughly beaten the whites they hated so. Emboldened by their success, they might now try to exterminate them all.

He hurried across the parade to Carrington's house. The Colonel had several of his officers with him. Black George admitted Paddock and Carrington shook his hand. "I was going to send for you. I want to talk to you about what happened yesterday."

Paddock asked, "Who's going out after the rest of the bodies, Colonel Carrington?"

"I am."

Captain Powell said, "You can't do that, Colonel. You're needed here."

"I won't order anyone to go. That means I'll have to go myself."

"Does anybody have to go? Can't we wait until we get some replacements from Fort Laramie?"

Carrington shook his head. "Those men deserve a decent burial." He turned his head and looked at Lt. Wands. "Lieutenant, I want you to take a detail of workmen and a twenty man guard, and go out to the cemetery to dig some graves. I want two graves, one large enough for Fetterman, Brown and Grummond, the other at least fifty feet long for the other men."

"Yes, sir. I'll get started on it right away. It looks like it might be going to storm."

"That's why I want to get the rest of those bodies as soon as possible. If it should snow, it might be impossible to find them all."

Paddock could see that Carrington had spent a sleepless night. The colonel was still profoundly shocked by what had happened yesterday. His hands shook and his face was pale.

Captain Ten Eyck, standing on the far side of the room, said, "I'll go with you, Colonel."

Lt. Matson said, "So will I."

"Thank you, gentlemen." He looked at Paddock. "Jess?"

Paddock nodded. "Sure, Colonel. I'll go."

Carrington nodded. "Then get the men ready, Captain Ten Eyck. I'll want about eighty, all mounted, and I'll want five ambulances to bring the bodies in. In addition, I want two howitzers and plenty of cannister shot for them."

"When will we leave?"

"When everything is ready, but I doubt if that will be much before eleven or twelve o'clock."

Ten Eyck, Wands and Matson saluted and left the room. Powell also excused himself. When they had gone, Carrington looked at Paddock. "You saw part of it, didn't you?" he asked.

Paddock shook his head. "Not really. I didn't see what finally happened to any of them. I saw them under attack, though, and it looked like it was pretty bad."

"You saw the bodies. Some of them had as many as thirty or forty arrows in them. Those men were captured alive and tortured, Jess. The arrows were shot into them after their clothes had been torn off by the Indians."

Paddock nodded. "I know, Colonel."

Carrington said feelingly, "The God-damned barbarous savages! Before we're through, we're going to have to kill them all."

CHAPTER 19

The column, under Colonel Carrington, did not leave Fort Kearny until about one o'clock. Captain Ten Eyck and Lt. Matson were with him, as was Jess Paddock. About half the men, eighty in all, were civilians, the others equally divided between infantry and cavalry. Also along was Dr. Elisha Gould, a civilian surgeon in the army's employ, for Dr. Hines was busy preparing for burial the bodies of the forty-nine brought in yesterday. Each had to be identified. Countless arrows had to be removed. The bodies had to be dressed in proper uniforms and in every case the cause of death must be listed on Surgeon Hines' report.

Proceeding slowly, the column crossed Big Piney Creek, which had again frozen over during the night. The wind was bitter cold and now and then a few flakes of snow stung the faces of the men.

At intervals, Carrington left pickets behind to advise him of any Indian action at his rear or against the fort and also to maintain signal communications with sentries at the fort.

It was late afternoon when the column finally reached the place where Captain Ten Eyck had loaded the forty-nine bodies yesterday. Still there had been no attack by the Indians although several hundred of them were visible in the valley of Peno Creek and on the east slope of Lodge Trail Ridge.

The column, with Carrington at its head, moved slowly along the ridge toward the rocks where the bodies of Wheatley, Fisher and Metzger, the bugler, were. Carrington's face turned paler when he saw the remaining bodies lying scattered on the slope. He motioned for the wagons to come on and to turn around when they reached the rocks.

Before ordering the bodies loaded into the wagons, Carrington took Ten Eyck, Matson and Paddock and rode among them. The mutilations here were even worse than those Paddock had witnessed yesterday. Eyes had been torn from their sockets and laid on rocks. Heads had been split open, the brains removed and also laid out on the rocks. Arms had been severed, skulls split. There were deliberate punctures, apparently made by knives while the victims were still alive, in every sensitive part of the bodies.

Carrington was shaking, both from shock and chill, as he ordered the bodies gathered up and placed in the wagons. Today, blankets had been brought to wrap them in, and every effort was made to match up the severed parts with the bodies from which they had been taken by the Indians.

While the work progressed, Carrington rode over the battlefield, his eyes on the ground, counting carefully each place where blood had been spilled, but from which the body of a killed or wounded Indian had been removed. Paddock accompanied him, also counting the bloodspots, but only those large enough to indicate the Indian who had made it had been killed. He counted sixty-five.

He said, "Colonel, Grummond's cavalry killed at least sixty-five Indians with their Spencers."

"What about the others? What about Fetterman's infantry?"

"Well, I looked around where we found their bodies yesterday and I don't think they did as well. They had those damned muzzle loading Springfields and I doubt if any of them got off more than a couple of shots. Some probably didn't get off but one."

Carrington frowned. "But how did it happen so quickly. How?"

Paddock said, "Too many Indians. Too

little experience on the part of the troops. I saw enough of it to tell that they were beaten from the start. Instead of finding cover and spreading out, they huddled together like sheep. You can see that for yourself in the way the bodies are bunched. They made it easy for the Indians."

Carrington said, "There'll be hell to pay over this."

Paddock nodded. He followed Carrington back to the road.

The colonel looked at him curiously. "Why was Grummond so far ahead of Fetterman?"

Paddock said, "Eagerness, I guess. O'Mara and I tried to get through to him and tell him to draw back and help Fetterman but we couldn't make it. There were several hundred Indians between us and Grummond's men."

"Was that when O'Mara was killed?"

"Yes, sir. If you don't mind, I'd like to go back and see if I can find his body."

"Go ahead, Jess. But don't get yourself killed."

Paddock rode back along the road. Light was already beginning to fade from the sky, which had been leaden gray all day. The wind still blew strong and cold out of the northwest and the flurries of snow were

210

more frequent than they had been earlier.

He heeled his horse into a steady trot. He passed the first of the pickets Carrington had left behind before he reached the spot where O'Mara had been killed.

His sorrel horse still lay where he had fallen but saddle and bridle had been removed. O'Mara's body was gone. The ground was covered with hoof prints, those of unshod ponies, and it was impossible to follow any single trail. It was as though O'Mara's body had disappeared into the air.

He circled around on the hillside below the road until it was too dark to see the ground. Then, shrugging regretfully, he returned to the road to wait for Carrington and his men.

They came down in darkness, the wagon wheels grating on the frozen ground, tug chains and singletrees clanking, the men cursing sourly at the cold and at the barbarity of the Indians. Paddock joined Carrington and the Colonel asked, "Find him, Jess?"

Paddock shook his head. "I don't know why they'd take his body but it looks like that's what they did."

"He'll probably never be found. There'll be nobody out on these hills for a long, long time."

Paddock nodded. It was possible that wolves had dragged O'Mara's body away during the night. It was also possible the Indians had dragged it away. At least, he thought, O'Mara had died before the Indians got to him. He had not been tortured as had so many of Fetterman's and Grummond's men.

Captain Ten Eyck asked, "What are you going to do now, Colonel?"

"Ready the fort for an Indian attack. Red Cloud probably thinks he'll never get a better chance than this to wipe us out. And I'll send a courier to Fort Laramie for reinforcements."

Paddock asked, "Want me to go, Colonel?"

Carrington shook his head. "Too risky, Jess. Mrs. Benedict would never forgive me if anything happened to you. I think I'll ask Portugee Phillips to go."

Paddock didn't argue the point with him. He knew there was little chance a courier could get through. The Indians would most certainly be watching the Bozeman Road between Fort Kearny and Fort Laramie.

But he didn't agree with Carrington that the fort was in jeopardy. He seriously doubted if the Indians would attack. Indians fought only when they could inflict heavy losses with little risk to themselves. They would not risk a frontal assault upon a fortified position, particularly when they knew how devastating the cannister shot of the artillery could be.

Still, Carrington's precautions were proper ones. The Colonel could not, in good conscience, do less than be prepared for the worst.

Once more it was a somber garrison that greeted the column's return to the fort. They lined the way on both sides of the gates, staring through the darkness at the loaded wagons. The wagons went directly across the parade to the post hospital and drew up there while Major Powell, Officer of the Day, detailed men to carry the bodies in.

It was almost ten o'clock. Paddock glimpsed Molly Benedict and rode straight to her. He dismounted and walked with her along the side of the parade toward her house. He left her at the stables long enough to care for his horse, then rejoined her in the dark and bitter wind.

It had turned much colder during the afternoon. Paddock guessed it must be near zero and would probably go to ten or twenty below tonight.

Molly's place was warm. He took off his

coat and sank wearily into a chair. Molly brought him coffee laced with whisky and he drank it gratefully. Her eyes were worried as she asked, "What's going to happen now? Will the Indians attack the fort?"

He shook his head. "I doubt it. They don't like that kind of fighting."

"Colonel Carrington thinks they will, doesn't he?"

Paddock nodded. "He does. But he has to think of every possibility."

"It's horrible! Eighty-one men!"

"Eighty-two. O'Mara's dead too."

"Did you find his body today?"

He shook his head.

She had some stew warming on the back of the stove and she brought him some of it. As soon as he had eaten, he kissed her and wearily went out into the everlasting wind. He could hear the shouts as the guard was changed. Otherwise the fort was dark and still.

Hearing voices, he stopped with his hand on his doorlatch. He saw two men come along the street, heading for the water gate.

They were talking as they passed and he recognized one voice as that of Colonel Carrington, the other as that of Portugee Phillips. Phillips was leading a horse, one that was instantly recognizable even in the dark as Colonel Carrington's own Kentucky thoroughbred.

Paddock called, "Good luck, Phillips."

Phillips waved a hand. Paddock went inside, thinking that Phillips must know how slight his chances were. But the bitter cold would help. Indian pickets stationed on the road would be more intent on staying warm than they would be on watching for anyone who might be escaping from the fort.

Paddock fell exhaustedly on the bed and pulled the covers over him. He was almost instantly asleep.

The Sioux did not attack the fort, apparently content with their decisive victory over Grummond and Fetterman. Portugee Phillips reached Fort Laramie on Christmas Day, and on January 17th, Lt. Col. Henry W. Wessels arrived at Fort Phil Kearny with two companies of the Second Cavalry and three of the Eighteenth Infantry, along with ammunition and supplies.

On January 23, Colonel Carrington, who had been relieved of his command by Brigadier General Philip St. George Cooke, left Fort Kearny for Fort Laramie, accompanied by his headquarters staff and the regimental band. The wives and children of men stationed at Kearny also went along. Sixty men accompanied the party as an escort. And in one of the wagons rode Molly Benedict and Jess Paddock.

The journey seemed endless and the hardships were unbelievable in deep snow and temperatures that sometimes reached forty below. But when Jess and Molly reached Fort Laramie they were married by the chaplain there.

And as soon as the weather moderated sufficiently, they continued southward in a light spring wagon Paddock had bought at Laramie.

There is, today, a place near Cheyenne where the grassland rolls away to infinity like the swells of a restless sea. A snug log ranchhouse nestles in a valley beside a clear and narrow stream. Here live the descendants of Jess and Molly Paddock.

Two graves, marked by small granite headstones, look out across the wind-swept land from the top of a nearby hill. The headstones face northward toward Fort Phil Kearny, now crumbled away and gone, and toward a ridge a few miles north of it where eighty-one men fought and died more than a hundred years ago. Massacre Ridge, it is called, in memory of the Fetterman tragedy.